"ISAAC, OH, ISAAC!" I CALLED JOYFULLY.

Isaac looked up in amazement at me and Melissa craning our necks over the edge of the roof. Then he saw the dog and took in the situation.

"Won't you call off your dog and let us get down, Isaac?" I said pleadingly.

Isaac stood and reflected for a moment or two. Then he came slowly forward and, before we realized what he was going to do, he took that ladder down and laid it on the ground.

"Isaac Appleby, what do you mean?" demanded Melissa wrathfully.

Isaac folded his arms and looked up. "I mean that you two women will stay up on the roof until one of you agrees to marry me," said Isaac solemnly.

I gasped.

"Isaac Appleby, you can't be in earnest?" I cried incredulously. "You couldn't be so mean?"

"I am in earnest. I want a wife, and I am going to have one. You two will stay up there, and Julius Caesar here will watch you until one of you makes up her mind to take me. You can settle it between yourselves, and let me know when you have come to a decision."

And with that Isaac walked jauntily into his new house.

The Doctor's Sweetheart
and other stories

L. M. MONTGOMERY

Selected and with an introduction by
Catherine McLay

BANTAM BOOKS
NEW YORK · TORONTO · LONDON · SYDNEY · AUCKLAND

RL 6, age 12 and up

The Doctor's Sweetheart and Other Stories

A Bantam Book/published by arrangement
with the author's estate.

The Starfire logo is a registered trademark of Bantam Books,
a division of Bantam Doubleday Dell Publishing Group, Inc.
Registered in U.S. Patent and Trademark Office and elsewhere.

Bantam edition/December 1993

ISBN 0-553-56330-0

Published simultaneously in the United States and Canada

Bantam Books are published by Bantam Books, a division of Bantam
Doubleday Dell Publishing Group, Inc. Its trademark, consisting of
the words "Bantam Books" and the portrayal of a rooster, is Regis-
tered in U.S. Patent and Trademark Office and in other countries.
Marca Registrada. Bantam Books, 1540 Broadway, New York, New
York 10036.

PRINTED IN THE UNITED STATES OF AMERICA

OPM   10 9 8 7 6 5 4

Table of Contents

Preface

I first became interested in the short stories of Lucy Maud Montgomery several years ago when I was approached by the editor of a small university press to edit a selection of her short stories not currently available in print. In the next few months, however, I discovered that her two original collections were still in print and that a third collection, edited by her son, had just recently appeared. I decided to search for stories which had been lost for years in files of old magazines and periodicals. I was surprised to learn that there were nearly 500 of these stories, although only twenty or so were indexed in The Readers Guide to Periodical Literature. During this search, I decided that the best audience for such a collection was the general public who have been reading and enjoying Montgomery's fiction for the past seventy years, and who are still buying current paperback and hardcover editions. This book, then, is dedicated to Montgomery readers everywhere.

The stories are arranged in chronological order and are reprinted from the following sources:

"Kismet," from *Canadian Magazine* 13, July 1899.

"Emily's Husband," from *Canadian Magazine* 22, November 1903.

"The Girl and the Wild Race," from *Era Magazine* 13, January 1904.

"The Promise of Lucy Ellen," from *The Delineator*, February 1904.

"The Parting of the Ways," from *Canadian Magazine*, February 1907.

"The Doctor's Sweetheart," from *Canadian Magazine*, June 1908.

"By Grace of Julius Caesar," from *Canadian Magazine*, September 1908.

"Akin to Love," from *Canadian Magazine* 34, December 1909.

"The Finished Story," from *Canadian Magazine*, December 1912.

"My Lady Jane," from *Maclean's Magazine*, February 1915.

"Abel and His Great Adventure," from *Canadian Magazine*, February 1917.

"The Garden of Spices," from *Maclean's Magazine*, March 1918.

"The Bride Is Waiting," from *Canadian Magazine*, April 1932.

"I Know a Secret," from *Good Housekeeping*, August 1935.

The stories have been printed as they appear in the original edition, except for correction of obvious typing errors and regularization of spelling and punctuation.

I would like to thank Dr. Stuart MacDonald, son and literary executor of L. M. Montgomery, for his kind permission to reprint these stories. I would also like to thank *Good Housekeeping* magazine and *Maclean's Magazine* for permission to use stories originally published in their magazines and Fitzhenry and Whiteside for permission to quote in the introduction from Montgomery's autobiography, *The Alpine Path*.

Introduction

Lucy Maúd Montgomery is best known in Canada and abroad for her twenty novels which depict the lives and adventures of adolescent girls and their initiation into adult society. With the publication of *Anne of Green Gables* in 1908, Montgomery soared to fame with six editions in the first six months and thirty-two American editions in five years. Today her novels have been translated into fifteen or more languages, including French, Spanish, Italian, Dutch, Finnish, Swedish, Norwegian, Danish, Polish, Icelandic, and Japanese. Over three million copies have appeared in British countries excluding Canada, and Anne has been the heroine of a silent film in 1919, a talking film by Hollywood in 1934, a British television adaption in 1972, and a musical in 1965, which played as far away as Japan during the World Fair in Osaka, 1970. Mark Twain, in a personal letter to Montgomery, called Anne "the dearest and most lovable child in fiction since the immortal Alice," and the British Prime Minister Ramsay Macdonald is quoted as remarking, "I've read every Montgomery book I could get my hands on." Several studies of Montgomery's life in relation to these novels have appeared since her death: the definitive biography by H. M. Ridley, *The Story of L. M. Montgomery*, in 1956; Mollie Gillen's fascinating account, *The Wheel of Things*, in 1975; and Francis W. P. Bolger's more specialized examination of her early career and her literary apprenticeship in *The Years Before Anne*, 1974. A recent film of her life by the Canadian Broadcasting Corporation dramatized her career and made use of material from her unpublished diaries.

Montgomery's short stories are less familiar than her novels or her life. Although her notebooks record the titles of over five hundred stories sold to magazines during her lifetime, less than fifty of these have been collected. In 1912 the publishers of *Anne of Green Gables* (1908) and its sequel *Anne of Avonlea* (1909) capitalized on their popularity to publish *Chronicles of Avonlea*, and in 1920 another collection, *Further Chronicles of Avonlea*. The stories had been printed from various magazines and periodicals of the time, and many were revised by Montgomery in 1911 to include settings near Avonlea and characters which appear in the novels. In 1973 Montgomery's son and literary executor Dr. Stuart Macdonald published *The Road to Yesterday*, a collection of fourteen stories dating from different periods of Montgomery's career and gathered together by her in the last year of her life. There remain, then, over four hundred stories to be located, in addition to twenty-five stories listed in indexes to periodical literature. In diary entries and in her letters to her friend Ephraim Weber, Montgomery refers to stories sold between 1900 and 1909 to *Smart Set, Ainslie's, Modern Women, Home Magazine, The American Home, Gunter's Magazine, McClure's Magazine,* and *Housewife,* among others. Later stories appeared in *The Canadian Magazine, Maclean's, The Delineator, Ladies' Home Journal, Canadian Home Journal,* and *Good Housekeeping*. The discovery of these stories will contribute greatly to our knowledge of Montgomery's early years as a writer and of the development of her talent.

The progress of Montgomery's literary apprenticeship is traced in her account of her life in *The Alpine Path,* in her letters and diaries, and in the three novels *Emily of New Moon, Emily Climbs,* and *Emily's Quest*. These novels Montgomery describes as her closest approach to autobiography, and they fictionalize several incidents from Montgomery's own life and literary experiences. In *The Alpine Path* she remarks:

I cannot remember the time when I was not writing, or when I did not mean to be an author. To write has always been my central purpose. . . . I was an indefatigable little scribbler, and stacks of manuscripts, long ago reduced to ashes, alas, bore testimony to the same. I wrote about all the little incidents of my existence. (pp. 52-3)

Her original ambition was to be a poet and at nine she wrote her first poem "Autumn," in imitation of Thompson's "The Seasons." But she inherited the blood of the story-teller from her great aunt Mary Lawson, many of whose oral tales were recorded by Montgomery in her own favourite work *The Story Girl*. Like her heroine Anne Shirley, Lucy Maud Montgomery formed a story club among her best friends, and like Anne, too, Lucy Maud wrote most of the plots. In these stories, she comments, "Almost everyone died." Her favourite story, "My Graves," recounted the tale of a minister's wife who buried a succession of children across the country from Newfoundland to Vancouver. Her first publications appeared during the year she spent with her father and stepmother in Prince Albert when she was sixteen — a poem "On Cape Le Force" in the Charlottetown *Daily Patriot* in November of 1890, a story "The Wreck of the Marco Polo" in the *Montreal Witness* in February of 1891, and a descriptive article on Saskatchewan in the Prince Albert *Times* in June of 1891. Like her later stories, "The Wreck of the Marco Polo" employed a setting in Prince Edward Island and recorded a time in the province's history.

In 1895, she published the sketch "Our Charivari" in a major magazine of the period, *Golden Days* of Philadelphia, and after this time references to stories become more frequent in her correspondence. Many of these were intended as juvenile stories for Sunday School papers, and Montgomery remarked in her diary:

I like doing these, but I should like it better if I didn't have to drag a moral into most of them. They won't sell without it, as a rule. So in the moral must go, broad or subtle, as suits the fibre of the particular editor I have in mind. The kind of juvenile story I like best to write — and read, too, for the matter of that — is a good, jolly one, "art for art's sake" or rather "fun for fun's sake," with no insidious moral hidden away in it like a pill in a spoonful of jam!

(quoted in Ridley, p. 75)

By 1901 she was beginning to appear in the better-known fashionable magazines, and from this time on she supported herself by her pen. Her letters between 1905 and 1909 refer to some twenty-five stories sold to various magazines in this period, as well as detailing the inception and development of *Anne of Green Gables* and *Anne of Avonlea*. Later correspondence indicates that her focus had shifted to the progress and success of the novels, and seven of the known stories of the twenties are parts of novels in the Emily series or *Magic for Marigold*. Most of the stories as well as the novels suggest that Montgomery wrote for a young audience. Of Anne she remarked to Ephraim Weber:

The book was written for *girls* and must please them to be a *financial* success. . . . Some day I shall try to write a book that satisfies me wholly. In a book for the young it wouldn't do to have the hero "fail tremendously", as you say. They couldn't understand or sympathize with that. It would take older people. I do not think I'll ever be able to write stories for mature people. My gift such as it is seems to lie along literature for the young. (p. 74)

The short story which perhaps comes closest to her intent is "The Brother Who Failed" in *Further Chronicles of Avonlea*. Her one experiment in full-length adult fiction, *A Tangled Web*, is a complex interweaving of the fortunes of several relatives awaiting the decision as to who will be the heir of rich and malicious old Aunt Becky.

Despite her vast popular audience, Montgomery has been frequently dismissed by critics with Ralph Connor and Nellie McClung as one of "the Sunshine School of Canadian Fiction," where "folk of good-natured innocence and simple-hearted faith defeat the spiteful and the stingy and the rude," and where "nobody ever suffers long or gets really hurt or says 'damn'." Montgomery was, however, very much aware of the issues of her time. She chose the form of romance rather than realism deliberately, as she suggests in the advice of Emily's teacher in *Emily Climbs*: "Live under your own hat. Don't be led away by these howls about realism. Remember pine woods are as real as pig-sties, and a darn sight pleasanter" (pp. 218-19). But while she uses the romance formula for most of her stories, she does deal with issues which are relevant today. Her predominant theme is marriage and its private and social expectations. Within this framework she examines such central problems as the demands of the individual versus those of the community, the demands of family relationships versus those of love, and the nature of marriage as personal fulfillment as opposed to economic necessity or to the duty to the family and society. She is also concerned with other themes: the search, particularly of women, for identity and stability, the needs of the life of the mind and the spirit, the duty of the artist to his own creativity as well as to the world, and his role in recording and even shaping the lives of others. Her characters live in communities where they are judged and even ridiculed. Clan relationships are complex and the family and community at times merge into one. There are conflict, jealousy, unhappiness, loss, self-sacrifice, and death.

The stories in this collection, like those of *Chronicles of Avonlea, Further Chronicles of Avonlea*, and *The Road to Yesterday*, are largely concerned with the theme of courtship. For the woman of Montgomery's fiction as for the woman of Jane Austen's day, the choice of a marriage partner was the central decision of her life which would determine not only her personal relationships, but also her role and status in society. On the role of women, Montgomery once commented to Weber:

> I believe anyone's sphere — whether man or woman — is where they can be happiest and do the best work. The majority of women are happiest and best placed at home, just as the majority of men are in the world. But there are exceptions to *both*. Some women are born for a public career. . . . And each has the right to fulfill the purpose of their birth. (p. 91)

Marriage, then, is the crisis in the lives of her heroines and serves as a focus for her comments on personal and social interaction. Several of these stories are conventional romances with appropriately happy endings, such as "The Girl and the Wild Race," "The Doctor's Sweetheart," "My Lady Jane," and "The Bride Is Waiting." "A Finished Story" is also traditional in completing an old romance through the discovery of the dead lover's diary. But "By Grace of Julius Caesar," although it too ends in marriage, is a parody of traditional romance in that the tone, the characters, and the crisis are comic and mundane. Several stories involve a late reunion after a separation in youth, a favourite Montgomery theme. In many of these stories the lovers are thirty or even forty years of age, and as in "Akin to Love" or "The Promise of Lucy Ellen," they must weigh the choice of marriage over stability, family obligations, or freedom, a choice which reflects the circumstances of Montgomery's own late marriage, her obligations to her grandmother and to her career. Two stories, "The Garden of Spices" and "I Know a Secret," end in marriage for secondary characters. Three stories deal with marital estrangement, but while "Kismet," "Emily's Husband," and "The Parting of the Ways" all end in reconciliation, only two can be considered to end happily.

The pattern of these stories follows the traditional pat-

13

tern of romantic comedy. The hero desires the heroine, his desire is blocked by certain persons or obstacles, and the dispelling of the block leads to a resolution in marriage. Perhaps the simplest of these stories is "My Lady Jane," which, although published in 1915, seems early in tone, style, and theme. Here the block between the lovers, arising from a misunderstanding of each other's character, is dispelled by a coincidence, Elliott Cameron's resemblance to his cousin Clark Oliver and the latter's invitation to replace him at a party at which the chief guest is Elliott's ex-sweetheart. In many stories the blocking character is frequently a parent or a relative who stands in place of a parent — an aunt, sister, or cousin. In "Emily's Husband" the couple are divided by the claims of both families, Stephen's mother and sister and Emily's brother and sister. In "The Girl and the Wild Race," Aunt Theodora opposes Judith's chosen suitor, and in "The Promise of Lucy Ellen," Cecily insists that her cousin must not desert her to marry an old suitor. Each of these stories is resolved by a decision of the protagonist. Emily defies her family and Stephen's sister when, in a moment of crisis, she recognizes her real love for him; Judith defies her aunt and promises to marry the first suitor to propose; and Cecily recognizes the price she has exacted of Lucy Ellen and renounces her claim. In each case the heroine has to weigh her responsibility to others against her responsibility to her own happiness.

In several other stories, the heroine is herself the blocking character. In "Kismet," the heroine's strong will, stubbornness, and dedication to a life in society prevent her from understanding her serious scholarly husband; the resolution comes with her acceptance of her need for him. In "The Garden of Spices," the division is similarly caused by the lady's pride and social status, compounded by a physical scar whose importance she overestimates in the eyes of her lover and the world. In "The Bride Is Waiting," Ellery must dispel the myth that Susan's heart is buried in France to win not only her hand but her love. And in "By Grace of Julius Caesar," Anne's rejection of Isaac is reversed by exceptional circumstances and by the quick thinking of the suitor, and the resolution is comic, in accord with the tone of parody. Perhaps the clearest example of the heroine as her own blocking character is "Akin to Love," where Josephine's decision to accept David arises not from outward circumstances or characters at all, but from her inward reconciliation of marriage to duty; although Montgomery suggests a certain irony here as indicated in her theme, "pity is akin to love," Josephine's conscious decision is to marry David because he needs her, not because she finds her life incomplete without him.

Two stories combine the theme of marriage with a secondary theme of the search of the artist for truth. In "The Parting of the Ways," young Stephen Gordon, on the point of leaving Canada to study art in Rome, imposes upon Beatrice Longworth his ideal of womanhood. To be true to this ideal, she renounces her lover and returns to her unhappy marriage. In "The Finished Story," a young writer alters the ending of an unhappy story to please an elderly lady and finds this ending is truer to life, as illustrated by her own story.

Another central theme in these stories is the search for identity and an understanding of the self. This search is frequently related to a choice in marriage, as it is in "Akin to Love." In two stories, the search is undertaken by a child. In "The Garden of Spices," Jims, ward of his uncle and a "half-aunt," seeks a mother replacement who can accept him for what he is and love his real self, not an idealized self. In "I Know a Secret," Jane Lawrence's fear that she is not herself but a daughter of the fisherman Six-Toed Jimmy leads to a new understanding of herself and her family as well as to a new social awareness. In "Abel and His Great Adventure," the young narrator learns, through old Abel's philosophy of acceptance with its consummation in death, to come to terms with his own needs and problems, as well as life itself.

Fate and coincidence play a major role in several stories. "Kismet" turns on fate as the title itself indicates. The reunion of husband and wife at the racecourse is due to chance, and her decision to return to him is also determined by chance — the victory of his horse over hers. Here Montgomery comments on the willingness of men to accept fate as a determinant in their lives. "My Lady Jane," similar in tone and style, turns not only on the coincidental likeness of Elliott Cameron and his cousin Clark Oliver, but also on the coincidence that Clark's intended is an old love of Elliott's. "The Finished Story" also turns on coincidence, the chance meeting of Sylvia Stanleymain with her dead lover's nephew and his discovery of his uncle's diary among his papers. The coincidence is made credible, at least in part, by the locale, by her return to the setting of the early romance, and by the young man's resemblance to her dead lover, which attracts her attention. "The Girl and the Wild Race" also depends in part on chance, for Aunt Theodora's chosen suitor, Ebon King, is away from home just at the time she sends for him to propose to Judith. In the end, however, the race is won not by the luckiest man, but by the hardiest and most daring. And in "I know a Secret," the hotel doctor who, in the absence of the local doctor, is called to attend to Jane in her sickness, is discovered to be an old lover of her mother's. Although coincidence is clearly employed at times as a device to further the plot, the range of her short stories indicate that, for Montgomery herself, fate or coincidence seemed to be a governing principle of the universe with the force of divine will.

The stories are carefully structured. The openings function to attract attention, arouse interest in theme and character, and open the action. The beginning of "The

Girl and the Wild Race" broaches the theme of marriage and its social implications:

> "If Judith would only get married," Mrs. Theodora Whitney was wont to sigh dolorously.
>
> Now there was no valid reason why Judith ought to get married unless she wanted to. But Judith was twenty-seven and Mrs. Theodora thought it was a terrible disgrace to be an old maid.
>
> "There has never been an old maid in our family so far back as we know of," she lamented. "And to think that there should be one now! It just drags us down to the level of the McGregors. They have always been noted for their old maids. . . . Your mother used to be dreadful proud of your good looks when you was a baby. I told her she needn't be. Nine times out of ten a beauty don't marry as well as an ordinary girl."

"The Promise of Lucy Ellen" opens with a situation which demands contradiction. Cecily's satisfaction with the "existing circumstances of her life" challenges interference, and the events of the story — the courtship of Lucy Ellen by an old suitor — turn Cecily's life upside down. "Emily's Husband" opens with a thumbnail sketch of Emily through the inflections of her voice: "It was very sweet always and very cold generally; sometimes it softened to tenderness with those she loved, but in it there was always an undertone of inflexibility and reserve." The voice reveals the pride which has led Emily to force her husband to choose between her and his mother and will not permit compromise even after the mother's death. The crisis of Stephen thus alters her personality; the voice which has never trembled now admits weakness and Emily's pride is defeated. The opening of "By Grace of Julius Caesar" sets the tone of the story as humourous and introduces the character of the narrator who controls the action.

The endings of Montgomery's stories are generally

happy, although the happiness is not always conventional or romantic. Despite her predilection for tragic endings, in her childish tales of "The Story Club," she clearly chose deliberately. As she has Emily remark in *Emily Climbs:*

> I read a story to-night. It ended unhappily. I was wretched until I invented a happy ending for it. I shall always end *my* stories happily. I don't care whether it's "true to life" or not. It's true to life as it *should be* and that's a better truth than the other.

Emily shared another experience with Montgomery herself. The editor had lost the ending of a story which had been running serially over a number of issues and Emily (and Lucy Maud) supplied the ending. In the novel, however, Montgomery satirizes the followers of artistic fashion. Emily later meets the author who bitterly remarks:

> I was angry — had I not a right to be? — and yet more sad than angry. My story was barbarously mutilated. *A happy ending.* Horrible. My ending was sorrowful and artistic. A happy ending can never be artistic.

The endings here are usually the conventional ones of marriage, as in "The Girl and the Wild Race," "My Lady Jane," "The Promise of Lucy Ellen," "The Doctor's Sweetheart," "Akin to Love," "By Grace of Julius Caesar," and "The Bride Is Waiting," or reconciliation, as in "Kismet" and "Emily's Husband." Yet "The Promise of Lucy Ellen," while it completes the romance of Lucy Ellen, destroys Cecily, and "The Parting of the Ways" ends in the retention of a marriage not for any reasons connected with the relationship, but to fulfill a young idealist's expectations of the heroine. Both "The Garden of Spices" and "I Know a Secret" end in the child's recognition of his/her identity and, central to the child's experience, the gaining of a parent replacement. "The Finished Story" completes a romance begun some forty years earlier. But "Abel and His

Great Adventure" is typical of another ending which Montgomery pursued, the coming of death, which brings not sadness but fulfillment and a sense of completion.

From the time of her first published story, "The Wreck of the Marco Polo," which describes the wreck of an old sailing vessel on Cavendish beach, Montgomery chose for her setting the Maritime region of Prince Edward Island. As she comments in her semi-autobiography *The Alpine Path*:

> . . . And yet we cannot define the charm of Prince Edward Island in terms of land or sea. It is too elusive — too subtle. Sometimes I have thought it was the touch of austerity in an Island landscape that gives it its peculiar charm. And whence comes that austerity? Is it in the dark dappling of spruce and fir? Is it in the glimpse of sea and river? Is it in the bracing tang of the salt air? Or does it go deeper still, down to the very soul of the land? For lands have personalities just as well as human beings; and to know that personality you must live in the land and companion it, and draw sustenance of body and spirit from it; so only can you really know a land and be known of it. (p. 11)

This is the landscape of most of her fiction, of the eight Anne books and the three Emily books, of *Pat of Silver Bush* and *Mistress Pat*, of *Magic for Marigold*, *The Tangled Web*, and half of *Jane of Lantern Hill*. Only *The Blue Castle* and a few short stories are set entirely in Ontario, where Montgomery lived for thirty years. Only one story, "Tannis of the Flats," makes use of her early Saskatchewan experience and the setting she admired so much is in the early essay "A Western Eden." For Montgomery, Prince Edward Island was truly "a region of the mind." Returning to it in later life, she was to say: "I felt that I *belonged* there — that I had done some violence to my soul when I left it." (Gillen, p. 137)

Chronicles of Avonlea and *Further Chronicles of Avonlea* are set in familiar territory, in the small towns and the countryside of Avonlea — the fictional Cavendish, White Sands, Grafton and East Grafton, Newbridge, Spencer, and Carmody. The stories in the present collection employ Island places less well known to Montgomery initiates — Woodford in "Emily's Husband," Oriental in "The Promise of Lucy Ellen," Harbour Light and Sweetwater in "A Finished Story," Stillwater in "Abel and His Great Adventure," Bartibog in "I Know a Secret," Broughton in "My Lady Jane," Meadowby in "Akin to Love," and an unidentified Maritime setting in "The Parting of the Ways." "Kismet" has no defined locale, apart from the racetrack, and "The Bride Is Waiting" is set in a small town or the outskirts of a city in Ontario, as is probably "The Garden of Spices."

In these narratives, the settings function to provide background, set the tone, complicate the action, reflect character, and symbolize the theme. In "Abel and His Great Adventure," an early description defines the mood and anticipates the ending. The sunset tones, the darkening shore, the ringing chapel bell, and the moan of the sea prepare for Abel's "great adventure," his journey through death, and reconcile the young narrator to an acceptance of Abel's philosophy of beauty. In "The Girl and the Wild Race," the setting complicates the action, the race between two suitors to propose to the heroine. It is the bold suitor who deserts the main road for a passage across treacherous creek ice and bared stumplands who wins the hand of the lady. And the season — winter moving into spring — symbolizes a new beginning for the heroine, a movement towards life.

The setting may also depict a journey of the mind or spirit. In "Emily's Husband," the storm, the raw air, and the writhing of the maples reflect the crisis in the mind of the protagonist Emily Fair, estranged from her husband

and suddently aware of his extreme illness. She recalls with fear the story of a dying soul on such a night "lost between earth and heaven," and makes a nightmare journey to her husband's bedside. The coming of the dawn and light marks the victory of life over death and love over pride. The storm in "I Know a Secret" is similar and reflects the conflict in the mind and heart of the child Jane Lawrence as she searches for her identity. The setting rapidly becomes demonic and the quest itself a descent into hell, as black clouds hang over the sea, lightning plays over the harbour, and the fishermen's houses are flooded with a lurid red light. The children playing on the sand, too, are demonic, threatening to trip Jane, drown her, or lock her in a house full of rats. Jane's discovery that she does not belong here after all opens her eyes to an appreciation of her own way of life; she has triumphed over both the storm and the mental conflict which have almost defeated her.

In these stories houses and gardens play a significant role and indicate Montgomery's love of place. Judith's preference for Bruce Marshall in "The Girl and the Wild Race" is in part determined by her attraction to his picturesque house with its gables and ivy, as opposed to the "bare intrusive grandeur" of Eben King's house. Anne's decision regarding Isaac in "By Grace of Julius Caesar" is influenced by the location of his house, and Josephine's acceptance of David in "Akin to Love" is only achieved after a careful weighing of the merits of her own cosy home "nestled between the grove of firs and the orchard," and David's need of her to rescue him from his sister's dirt and disorder. The buying and furnishing of a house in "The Bride Is Waiting" reveals to Susan the true nature of her feelings for Ellery; in this discovery the garden plays a significant part. The garden setting is most central in "Abel and His Great Adventure," where it plays an important role in Abel's philosophy of life, and in "The Garden of Spices," where the garden is truly a "secret garden" not only for Jims but for Miss Avery, and suggests the enchantment of the sleeping beauty.

In each of these fourteen stories, the point of view has been chosen carefully to suit the theme and to mould our reactions to events and characters. Several stories are told from the author's omniscient viewpoint to encourage detachment and objectivity and to allow us to observe the action from several angles. In "Kismet," the detachment of the author balances the subjectivity of the heroine and prepares for the tone of fatalism in the ending. In "The Parting of the Ways," we see the possible elopement of Beatrice Longworth from the angle of the village, of Beatrice herself and of young Stephen Gordon; thus we are aware of the consequences of Stephen's idealism but not its cost. We sympathize with Judith in "The Girl and the Wild Race," but we are not limited to her vision; we see the race from beginning to end as Judith herself cannot do.

The choice of the first person as narrator (where the story is told by "I") allows us to identify with one particular point of view and to become involved in the action, as in "My Lady Jane." The narrator in "By Grace of Julius Caesar" is both participant and observer, and it is the conflict between these two roles which leads both to the tension and to the humour. The young male narrators in "The Finished Story" and "Abel and His Great Adventure" are also both observers and participants. From Miss Sylvia the young writer learns about the nature of love, and from old Abel the young schoolmaster learns a basic philosophy of acceptance and content which alters his whole life. The narrator in "The Doctor's Sweetheart" is wholly an observer, but her presence adds interest to an otherwise rather sentimental romance and widens the theme to comment on the need of the elderly to live vicariously through the experiences and involvements of the young around them.

Six of the stories combine these two points of view; we see largely through the eyes and experience of the protago-

22

nist, but the author is also free to make us aware of his or her limitations. Thus we are dramatically involved with the situations of Cecily Foster in "The Promise of Lucy Ellen," Emily Fair in "Emily's Husband," Josephine in "Akin to Love," and Susan in "The Bride Is Waiting," but we are also able to see blindnesses of which they are unaware — their vulnerability, their pride, and the surface wit which masks an insecurity and a longing for deep human attachment. In two stories, "The Garden of Spices" and "I Know a Secret," we share with Jims and Jane as detached observers of the adult world of conflict, jealousy, and love, and yet participate in the child's world of insecurity, tension, even hostility. Here, as in her novels of the young Anne, Emily, Pat, Marigold, and Jane, Montgomery vividly recalls for us the doubts, fears, and intensified perceptions of our own childhood experiences and emotions.

Montgomery's strong sense of humour, sometimes wry and frequently ironic, is evident in these stories in the plotting and handling of incident, in the depiction of characters, and in the control of dialogue. "By Grace of Julius Caesar" turns on humour of incident. A trivial event — the intervention of an ill-mannered dog — leads to marriage, and the absurdity of the situation is heightened by the comic dialogue and flat tone. We gradually realize with the narrator the discrepancy between her romantic inclinations and the prosaic, even farcical, events which lead to her acceptance. "My Lady Jane" also employs humour of situation. Here Montgomery used the old comic device of the double to create dramatic irony, where the audience and the narrator share in a knowledge which none of the other characters possess. Part of the humour, however, consists in our recognition of the narrator's character, his essential stuffiness, even while we sympathize with him. We see his pompousness in such remarks as "he was a bit of a cad, and stupider than anyone belonging to our family had any right to be" or "It is always rather nice to be able to pity a person you dislike," yet they coincide with our own private views of ourselves and our relations. In several stories which involve middle-aged brides, the heroines retain a sense of detachment and an awareness of the ludicrousness of the situation, even though they are becoming conscious of their own vulnerability. In "Akin to Love," for example, Josephine roundly asserts that she has no need of a marriage in general and of David in particular, but quickly justifies her decision to accept David with the defence: "It's my duty, plain and clear, to come here and make things pleasant for him — the pointing of Providence, as you might say," adding, with characteristic understatement: "The worst of it is, I'll have to tell him so myself. He'll never dare to mention the subject again." The humour here, as in "The Bride Is Waiting," "The Promise of Lucy Ellen," and "By Grace of Julius Caesar," lies in our recognition that the heroine uses wit as a mask to hide behind, and we watch her reveal her real desires behind her professed ones. These stories effectively employ irony; what is asserted by the narrator differs from the underlying meaning conveyed by the author herself. Montgomery also conveys a strong sense of irony in "Kismet," "Emily's Husband," "The Girl and the Wild Race," and "The Parting of the Ways."

Essentially a regionalist, L. M. Montgomery placed Prince Edward Island on the map, as attested to by the many thousands of pilgrims who visit Green Gables from all over the world. Through her heroine Emily Starr in *Emily Climbs*, Montgomery expresses her own ambition. Emily is advised by her teacher to remain in Canada and to write, like Charlotte Brontë, of her own time and place: "That's what I wanted you to be — pure Canadian through and through, doing something as far as in you lay for the literature of your own country, keeping your Canadian tang and flavour." And to Janet Royal's persuasions that she move to New York for "you'll never be able to write anything really worth while here — no big thing," Emily replies:

> I'll create my own atmosphere. . . . And as for material — people *live* here just the same as anywhere else — suffer and enjoy and sin and aspire just as they do in New York. . . . I know life is rather cramped here in some ways — but the sky is as much mine as anybody's. I may not succeed here — but, if not, I wouldn't succeed in New York either. Some fountain of living water would dry up in my soul.

But Montgomery is more than a regionalist. As one critic, Elizabeth Waterson, notes, she expresses in her stories and novels "the recurring myths of girlhood," the archetypal patterns of experience which are still evident today. In an article "The Teen-Age Girl," published in *Chatelaine* March 1931, Montgomery remarks:

> I have, I believe, managed to retain even till now a very vivid recollection of what I was, and what I wished to be and how far and why I failed. For girlhood and its problems do not change as much from generation to generation as folks imagine. The outward fashion changes, but underneath they remain basically the same.

Her heroines, Anne, Emily, Pat, Jane, and Marigold still appeal today, as indicated by current reprints of all the Montgomery novels.

The stories in this collection indicate Montgomery's concern with "lives of girls and women." But they also suggest a wider range of themes and styles than is evident in her twenty novels for girls. In these days of new interest in women's themes and women writers, we may come to see Montgomery not merely as a teller of simple girl's stories, but as the conscious literary artist and craftsman that she strove all her life to be.

BOOKS AND ARTICLES ON
L. M. MONTGOMERY

Montgomery, L. M. *The Alpine Path: The Story of My Career*. Toronto: Fitzhenry and Whiteside, 1974.

Eggleston, Wilfred, ed. *The Green Gables Letters* from L. M. Montgomery to Ephraim Weber, 1905-1909. Toronto: Ryerson, 1960.

Anonymous. *Lucy Maud Montgomery, The Island's Lady of Stories*, Women's Institute, Springfield, Charlottetown, 1964.

Bolger, Francis P. *The Years Before "Anne"*. Prince Edward Island Heritage Foundation, 1974.

Gillen, Mollie. *The Wheel of Things, A Biography of L. M. Montgomery*. Toronto: Fitzhenry and Whiteside, 1975; also, "Maud Montgomery: The Girl Who Wrote Green Gables" in *Chatelaine*, July 1973.

Ridley, Hilda M. *The Story of L. M. Montgomery*. 1956. Reprint Toronto: McGraw-Hill Ryerson, 1973.

Sclanders, Ian. "Lucy of Green Gables." *Macleans' Magazine*, Dec. 15, 1951.

Waterson, Elizabeth. "Lucy Maud Montgomery." In *The Clear Spirit: Twenty Canadian Women and Their Times*, edited by Mary Quayle Innis. Toronto: University of Toronto Press, 1966.

BIOGRAPHY: L. M. MONTGOMERY (MRS. EWEN MACDONALD)

1874—born November 30 at Clifton (New London), Prince Edward Island. Daughter of Hugh John Montgomery and Clara Woolner Macneill. Her great great grandfather Hugh Montgomery emigrated from Scotland to Prince Edward Island in 1769, and her great great grandfather John Macneill emigrated from Argyleshire in 1775.

1876—September: death by pneumonia of her mother, Clara Montgomery. Lucy Maud was brought up by her grandparents Alexander and Lucy Macneill in Cavendish. Her father moved shortly after to Prince Albert, Saskatchewan, where he settled permanently in 1881. He worked for the Department of the Interior for several years and also ran a real estate agency and auctioneering service.

1880—began to attend school at Cavendish.

1882-5—the Macneills took in two boarders, Wellington and Dave Nelson (ages 8 and 7).

1884—wrote her first poem, "Autumn"; she also began a diary about this time and continued it for fifty-five years.

1890—in August she accompanied her grandfather Montgomery to visit her father in Prince Albert and remained there for the winter with his wife (Mary Ann MacRae, married 1887), his daughter Katie, and his son Bruce. Two later children of the marriage were Hugh and Ila May.

—first publication in verse, "On Cape Le Force," in *The Daily Patriot* of Charlottetown, November 26.

1891—first story "The Wreck of the Marco Polo" published in the Montreal *Witness*, February 1891, and copied in Charlottetown *Daily Patriot*, March 11.

—descriptive article on Saskatchewan, "A Western Eden"

in Prince Albert *Times,* June 1891, and copied by other
western papers.

—returned to Cavendish on September 4 and spent the
winter with her Aunt Annie and Uncle John Campbell
at Park Corners.

1893— attended Prince of Wales Colleges in Charlottetown and
-4 studied for a teaching licence.

1894— taught school at Bideford, Prince Edward Island, and
-5 lodged at the Methodist parsonage.

1895— attended Dalhousie College in Halifax, where she
-6 studied English Language and Literature under Archibald MacMechan. During one week she had three acceptances, a short story for *Golden Days,* an essay for the Halifax *Evening Mail,* and a poem for *Youth's Companion.* Her essay "Portia — A Study" was chosen to be read at the Convocation Exercises at the Opera House, June 9, 1896. Her essay "A Girl's Place at Dalhousie College" was published in the *Halifax Herald,* April 1896.

1896— taught school at Belmont, P.E.I.
-7

1897— taught school at Lower Bedeque, P.E.I.
-8 death of Grandfather Macneill in March. She returned to Cavendish to live with her grandmother for the next thirteen years until her grandmother's death (except for several months in 1901-2).

1898— in the next three years she assisted with the Post Office,
-1901 managed the household, and wrote. By 1901 she was making a "liveable income" from her writing and had been accepted by such magazines as *The Delineator, Smart Set,* and *Ainslie's.*

1900— death by pneumonia of her father on January 16.

1901— in the autumn she moved to Halifax and took a position on the staff of the *Daily Echo,* the evening edition of the Halifax *Chronicle.* She edited the page of "Society Letters," some of which she also wrote, and wrote a column "Around the Tea-Table" under the pseudonym of Cynthia.

1902— returned to her grandmother's home at Cavendish and continued writing.

1903—met her future husband Reverend Ewen Macdonald, who was the Presbyterian minister at Cavendish.

1904
-5 —began *Anne of Green Gables* in the spring of 1904 and completed it in October of 1905. It was refused by several publishers and she put it away in a cupboard.

1906—engagement to Ewen Macdonald. The couple could not be married immediately as Montgomery had promised to remain with her grandmother.

1907—*Anne of Green Gables* accepted by L. C. Page of Boston.

1908—published *Anne of Green Gables*; in the next six months it went through six editions. In February of 1909 she received her first royalty cheque of $1730 on 19,000 copies at 9¢ a copy.
—she began a sequel, *Anne of Avonlea*.

1909—published *Anne of Avonlea*.

1910—published *Kilmeny of the Orchard*, written several years previously and published under another title as a serial in an American magazine.

1911—published *The Story Girl*.
—death of Grandmother Macneill in March at age 87 and she moved to the home of Uncle John Campbell of Park Corners.

—July 5 — marriage to Reverend Ewen Macdonald and honeymoon in the British Isles.

—September — to Leaskdale, Ontario, where Rev. Macdonald had been Presbyterian minister since March of 1910 and settled into the Manse. At a reception at the Toronto Branch of the Canadian Women's Press Club she met another new bride, Mrs. Donald McGregor (Marian Keith) who had also published four novels to date. They remained lifelong friends.

1912—July 7 — birth of Chester Cameron.
—published *Chronicles of Avonlea*, stories collected from magazines.

1913—published *The Golden Road*.

1914—August 13 — birth of Hugh, who lived only one day.

1915—published *Anne of the Island*.
—October 7 — birth of Stuart.

1916—published *The Watchman and Other Poems*, her only book of poetry.

1917—published *Anne's House of Dreams*.

1919—published *Rainbow Valley*.

1920—L. C. Page published *Further Chronicles of Avonlea*, a collection of stories previously published in magazines, without Montgomery's permission. A suit followed which lasted for 9 years. Montgomery won the case, but received little recompense.

1921—published *Rilla of Ingleside*.

—Hollywood silent version of *Anne of Green Gables* set in the United States. Montgomery received no royalties.

1923—published *Emily of New Moon*, the most autobiographical of her books.

1925—published *Emily Climbs*.

—moved to Norval, Ontario, to the Presbyterian Manse.

1926—published *The Blue Castle*.

1927—published *Emily's Quest*.

1929—published *Magic for Marigold*.

1931—published *A Tangled Web*. (British edition titled *Aunt Becky Began*).

1932—published *Pat of Silver Bush*.

1935—published *Mistress Pat*.

—the increasing ill health of Ewen Macdonald led to their retirement from the Church. They settled in Toronto on Riverside Drive where Chester and Stuart could attend courses in law and medicine.

—was made an Officer of the Order of the British Empire by King George. She was also a Fellow of the Royal Society of Arts and Letters of England, a member of the Canadian Author's Association, the Canadian Women's Press Club, and the Literary and Artistic Institute of France, which presented her with a silver medal for her literary style.

1936—published *Anne of Windy Poplars*.

1937—published *Jane of Lantern Hill*.

1938—suffered from a setback in health from which she never completely recovered.

1939—published *Anne of Ingleside*.

1942—died on Friday April 24. She was buried in Prince Edward Island in a grave overlooking the house called Green Gables.

1943—death of Reverend Ewen Macdonald and burial beside his wife.

1965—musical *Anne of Green Gables* on stage in Charlottetown.

1974—publication by her son Stuart Macdonald of *The Road to Yesterday*, a collection of short stories from her manuscripts.

1979—publication of *The Doctor's Sweetheart and Other Stories*.

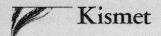

Kismet

The fifth heat in the free-for-all was just over. "Lu-Lu" had won, and the crowd on the grand stand and the hangers-on around the track were cheering themselves hoarse. Clear through the noisy clamour shrilled a woman's cry.

"Ah — I have dropped my scorecard."

A man in front of her turned.

"I have an extra one, madame. Will you accept it?"

Her small, modishly-gloved hand closed eagerly on it before she lifted her eyes to his face. Both started convulsively. The man turned very pale, but the woman's ripe-tinted face coloured darkly.

"You?" she faltered.

His lips parted in the coldly-grave smile she remembered and hated.

"You are not glad to see me," he said calmly, "but that, I suppose, was not to be expected. I did not come here to annoy you. This meeting is as unexpected to me as to you. I had no suspicion that for the last half-hour I had been standing next to my—"

She interrupted him by an imperious gesture. Still clutching the scorecard she half-turned from him. Again he smiled, this time with a tinge of scorn, and shifted his eyes to the track.

None of the people around them had noticed the little by-play. All eyes were on the track, which was being cleared for the first heat of another race. The free-for-all horses were being led away blanketed. The crowd cheered "Lu-Lu" as she went past, a shapeless oddity. The backers of "Mascot", the rival favourite, looked gloomy.

The woman noticed nothing of all this. She was small, very pretty, still young, and gowned in a quite unmistakable way. She studied the man's profile furtively. He looked older than when she had seen him last — there were some silver threads gleaming in his close-clipped dark hair and short, pointed beard. Otherwise there was little change in the quiet features and somewhat stern grey eyes. She wondered if he had cared at all.

They had not met for five years. She shut her eyes and looked in on her past. It all came back very vividly. She had been eighteen when they were married — a gay, high-spirited girl and the season's beauty. He was much older and a quiet, serious student. Her friends had wondered why she married him — sometimes she wondered herself, but she had loved him, or thought so.

The marriage had been an unhappy one. She was fond of society and gaiety, he wanted quiet and seclusion. She was impulsive and impatient, he deliberate and grave. The strong wills clashed. After two years of an unbearable sort of life they had separated — quietly, and without scandal of any sort. She had wanted a divorce, but he would not agree to that, so she had taken her own independent fortune and gone back to her own way of life. In the following five years she had succeeded in burying all remembrance well out of sight. No one knew if she were satisfied or not; her world was charitable to her and she lived a gay and quite irreproachable life. She wished that she had not come to the races. It was such an irritating encounter. She opened her eyes wearily; the dusty track, the flying horses, the gay dresses of the women on the grandstand, the cloudless blue sky, the brilliant September sunshine, the purple distances all commingled in a glare that made her head ache. Before it all she saw the tall figure by her side, his face turned from her, watching the track intently.

She wondered with a vague curiosity what induced him to come to the races. Such things were not greatly in his line. Evidently their chance meeting had not disturbed him. It was a sign that he did not care. She sighed a little wearily and closed her eyes. When the heat was over he turned to her.

"May I ask how you have been since—since we met last? You are looking extremely well. Has Vanity Fair palled in any degree?"

She was angry at herself and him. Where had her careless society manner and well-bred composure gone? She felt weak and hysterical. What if she should burst into tears before the whole crowd — before those coldly critical grey eyes? She almost hated him.

"No — why should it? I have found it very pleasant — and I have been well — very well. And you?"

He jotted down the score carefully before he replied.

"I? Oh, a book-worm and recluse always leads a placid life. I never cared for excitement, you know. I came down here to attend a sale of some rare editions, and a well-meaning friend dragged me out to see the races. I find it rather interesting, I must confess, much more so than I should have fancied. Sorry I can't stay until the end. I must go as soon as the free-for-all is over, if not before. I have backed 'Mascot'; you?"

" 'Lu-Lu' " she answered quickly — it almost seemed defiantly. How horribly unreal it was — this carrying on of small talk, as if they were the merest of chance-met acquaintances! "She belongs to a friend of mine, so I am naturally interested."

"She and 'Mascot' are ties now — both have won two heats. One more for either will decide it. This is a good day for the races. Excuse me."

He leaned over and brushed a scrap of paper from her grey cloak. She shivered slightly.

"You are cold! This stand is draughty."

"I am not at all cold, thank you. What race is this? — oh! the three-minute one."

She bent forward with assumed interest to watch the

scoring. She was breathing heavily. There were tears in her eyes — she bit her lips savagely and glared at the track until they were gone.

Presently he spoke again, in the low, even tone demanded by circumstances.

"This is a curious meeting, is it not? — quite a flavor of romance! By-the-way, do you read as many novels as ever?"

She fancied there was mockery in his tone. She remembered how very frivolous he used to consider her novel-reading. Besides, she resented the personal tinge. What right had he?

"Almost as many," she answered carelessly.

"I was very intolerant, wasn't I?" he said after a pause. "You thought so — you were right. You have been happier since you—left me?"

"Yes," she said defiantly, looking straight into his eyes.

"And you do not regret it?"

He bent down a little. His sleeve brushed against her shoulder. Something in his face arrested the answer she meant to make.

"I—I—did not say that," she murmured faintly.

There was a burst of cheering. The free-for-all horses were being brought out for the sixth heat. She turned away to watch them. The scoring began, and seemed likely to have no end. She was tired of it all. It didn't matter a pin to her whether "Lu-Lu" or "Mascot" won. What *did* matter! Had Vanity Fair after all been a satisfying exchange for love? He *had* loved her once, and they had been happy at first. She had never before said, even in her own heart: "I am sorry," but—suddenly, she felt his hand on her shoulder, and looked up. Their eyes met. He stooped and said almost in a whisper:

"Will you come back to me?"

"I don't know," she whispered breathlessly, as one half-fascinated.

"We were both to blame — but I the most. I was too hard on you — I ought to have made more allowance. We are wiser now both of us. Come back to me—my wife."

His tone was cold and his face expressionless. It was on her lips to cry out "No," passionately.

But the slender, scholarly hand on her shoulder was trembling with the intensity of his repressed emotion. He *did* care, then. A wild caprice flashed into her brain. She sprang up.

"See," she cried, "they're off now. This heat will probably decide the race. If 'Lu-Lu' wins I will not go back to you, if 'Mascot' does I will. That is my decision."

He turned paler, but bowed in assent. He knew by bitter experience how unchangeable her whims were, how obstinately she clung to even the most absurd.

She leaned forward breathlessly. The crowd hung silently on the track. "Lu-Lu" and "Mascot" were neck and neck, getting in splendid work. Half-way round the course "Lu-Lu" forged half a neck ahead, and her backers went mad. But one woman dropped her head in her hands and dared look no more. One man with white face and set lips watched the track unswervingly.

Again "Mascot" crawled up, inch by inch. They were on the home stretch, they were equal, the cheering broke out, then silence, then another terrific burst, shouts, yells and clappings — "Mascot" had won the free-for-all. In the front row a woman stood up, swayed and shaken as a leaf in the wind. She straightened her scarlet hat and readjusted her veil unsteadily. There was a smile on her lips and tears in her eyes. No one noticed her. A man beside her drew her hand through his arm in a quiet proprietary fashion. They left the grand stand together.

Emily's Husband

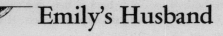

Emily Fair got out of Hiram Jameson's wag-
gon at the gate. She took her satchel and parasol and, in
her clear, musical tones, thanked him for bringing her
home. Emily had a very distinctive voice. It was very sweet
always and very cold generally; sometimes it softened to
tenderness with those she loved, but in it there was always
an undertone of inflexibility and reserve. Nobody had ever
heard Emily Fair's voice tremble.

"You are more than welcome, Mrs. Fair," said Hiram
Jameson, with a glance of bold admiration. Emily met it
with an unflinching indifference. She disliked Hiram
Jameson. She had been furious under all her external
composure because he had been at the station when she
left the train.

Jameson perceived her scorn, but chose to disregard it.

"Proud as Lucifer," he thought as he drove away. "Well,
she's none the worse of that. I don't like your weak women
—they're always sly. If Stephen Fair don't get better she'll
be free and then—"

He did not round out the thought, but he gloated over
the memory of Emily, standing by the gate in the harsh,
crude light of the autumn sunset, with her tawny, brown
hair curling about her pale, oval face and the scornful glint
in her large, dark-grey eyes.

Emily stood at the gate for some time after Jameson's
waggon had disappeared. When the brief burst of sunset
splendour had faded out she turned and went into
the garden where late asters and chrysanthemums still
bloomed. She gathered some of the more perfect ones here
and there. She loved flowers, but to-night the asters seemed

38

to hurt her, for she presently dropped those she had gathered and deliberately set her foot on them.

A sudden gust of wind came over the brown, sodden fields and the ragged maples around the garden writhed and wailed. The air was raw and chill. The rain that had threatened all day was very near. Emily shivered and went into the house.

Amelia Phillips was bending over the fire. She came forward and took Emily's parcels and wraps with a certain gentleness that sat oddly on her grim personality.

"Are you tired? I'm glad you're back. Did you walk from the station?"

"No. Hiram Jameson was there and offered to drive me home. I'd rather have walked. It's going to be a storm, I think. Where is John?"

"He went to the village after supper," answered Amelia, lighting a lamp. "We needed some things from the store."

The light flared up as she spoke and brought out her strong, almost harsh features and deep-set black eyes. Amelia Phillips looked like an overdone sketch in charcoal.

"Has anything happened in Woodford while I've been away?" asked Emily indifferently. Plainly she did not expect an affirmative answer. Woodford life was not eventful.

Amelia glanced at her sharply. So she had not heard! Amelia had expected that Hiram Jameson would have told her. She wished that he had, for she never felt sure of Emily. The older sister knew that beneath that surface reserve was a passionate nature, brooking no restraint when once it overleaped the bounds of her Puritan self-control. Amelia Phillips, with all her naturally keen insight and her acquired knowledge of Emily's character, had never been able to fathom the latter's attitude of mind towards her husband. From the time that Emily had come back to her girlhood's home, five years before, Stephen Fair's name had never crossed her lips.

"I suppose you haven't heard that Stephen is very ill," said Amelia slowly.

Not a feature of Emily's face changed. Only in her voice when she spoke was a curious jarring, as if a false note had been struck in a silver melody.

"What is the matter with him?"

"Typhoid," answered Amelia briefly. She felt relieved that Emily had taken it so calmly. Amelia hated Stephen Fair with all the intensity of her nature because she believed that he had treated Emily ill, but she had always been distrustful that Emily in her heart of hearts loved her husband still. That, in Amelia Phillips' opinion, would have betrayed a weakness not to be tolerated.

Emily looked at the lamp unwinkingly.

"That wick needs trimming," she said. Then, with a sudden recurrence of the untuneful note:

"Is he dangerously ill?"

"We haven't heard for three days. The doctors were not anxious about him Monday, though they said it was a pretty severe case."

A faint, wraith-like change of expression drifted over Emily's beautiful face and was gone in a moment. What was it — relief? Regret? It would have been impossible to say. When she next spoke her vibrant voice was as perfectly melodious as usual.

"I think I will go to bed, Amelia. John will not be back until late I suppose, and I am very tired. There comes the rain. I suppose it will spoil all the flowers. They will be beaten to pieces."

In the dark hall Emily paused for a moment and opened the front door to be cut in the face with a whip-like dash of rain. She peered out into the thickly gathering gloom. Beyond, in the garden, she saw the asters tossed about, phantom-like. The wind around the many-cornered old farmhouse was full of wails and sobs.

The clock in the sitting-room struck eight. Emily shivered and shut the door. She remembered that she had been married at eight o'clock that very morning seven years ago. She thought she could see herself coming down

40

the stairs in her white dress with her bouquet of asters. For a moment she was glad that those mocking flowers in the garden would be all beaten to death before morning by the lash of wind and rain.

Then she recovered her mental poise and put the hateful memories away from her as she went steadily up the narrow stairs and along the hall with its curious slant as the house had settled, to her own room under the north-western eaves.

When she had put out her light and gone to bed she found that she could not sleep. She pretended to believe that it was the noise of the storm that kept her awake. Not even to herself would Emily confess that she was waiting and listening nervously for John's return home. That would have been to admit a weakness, and Emily Fair, like Amelia, despised weakness.

Every few minutes a gust of wind smote the house, with a roar as of a wild beast, and bombarded Emily's window with a volley of rattling drops. In the silences that came between the gusts she heard the soft, steady pouring of the rain on the garden paths below, mingled with a faint murmur that came up from the creek beyond the barns where the pine boughs were thrashing in the storm. Emily suddenly thought of a weird story she had once read years before and long forgotten — a story of a soul that went out in a night of storm and blackness and lost its way between earth and heaven. She shuddered and drew the counterpane over her face.

"Of all things I hate a fall storm most," she muttered. "It frightens me."

Somewhat to her surprise — for even her thoughts were generally well under the control of her unbending will — she could not help thinking of Stephen — thinking of him not tenderly or remorsefully, but impersonally, as of a man who counted for nothing in her life. It was so strange to think of Stephen being ill. She had never known him to have a day's sickness in his life before. She looked back

41

over her life much as if she were glancing with a chill interest at a series of pictures which in no way concerned her. Scene after scene, face after face, flashed out on the background of the darkness.

Emily's mother had died at her birth, but Amelia Phillips, twenty years older than the baby sister, had filled the vacant place so well and with such intuitive tenderness that Emily had never been conscious of missing a mother. John Phillips, too, the grave, silent, elder brother, loved and petted the child. Woodford people were fond of saying that John and Amelia spoiled Emily shamefully.

Emily Phillips had never been like the other Woodford girls and had no friends of her own age among them. Her uncommon beauty won her many lovers, but she had never cared for any of them until Stephen Fair, fifteen years her senior, had come a-wooing to the old, gray, willow-girdled Phillips homestead.

Amelia and John Phillips never liked him. There was an ancient feud between the families that had died out among the younger generation, but was still potent with the older.

From the first Emily had loved Stephen. Indeed, deep down in her strange, wayward heart, she had cared for him long before the memorable day when he had first looked at her with seeing eyes and realized that the quiet, unthought-of child who had been growing up at the old Phillips place had blossomed out into a woman of strange, seraph-like beauty and deep grey eyes whose expression was nevermore to go out of Stephen Fair's remembrance from then till the day of his death.

John and Amelia Phillips put their own unjustifiable dislike of Stephen aside when they found that Emily's heart was set on him. The two were married after a brief courtship and Emily went out from her girlhood's home to the Fair homestead, two miles away.

Stephen's mother lived with them. Janet Fair had never liked Emily. She had not been willing for Stephen to marry her. But, apart from this, the woman had a natural, ineradicable love of making mischief and took a keen pleasure in it. She loved her son and she had loved her husband, but nevertheless, when Thomas Fair had been alive she had fomented continual strife and discontent between him and Stephen. Now it became her pleasure to make what trouble she could between Stephen and his wife.

She had the advantage of Emily in that she was always sweet-spoken and, on the surface, sweet-tempered. Emily, hurt and galled in a score of petty ways, so subtle that they were beyond a man's courser comprehension, astonished her husband by her fierce outbursts of anger that seemed to him for the most part without reason or excuse. He tried his best to preserve the peace between his wife and mother; and when he failed, not understanding all that Emily really endured at the elder woman's merciless hands, he grew to think her capricious and easily irritated — a spoiled child whose whims must not be taken too seriously.

To a certain extent he was right. Emily had been spoiled. The unbroken indulgence which her brother and sister had always accorded her had fitted her but poorly to cope with the trials of her new life. True, Mrs. Fair was an unpleasant woman to live with, but if Emily had chosen to be more patient under petty insults, and less resentful of her husband's well-meant though clumsy efforts for harmony, the older woman could have effected real little mischief. But this Emily refused to be, and the breach between husband and wife widened insidiously.

The final rupture came two years after their marriage. Emily, in rebellious anger, told her husband that she would no longer live in the same house with his mother.

"You must choose between us," she said, her splendid voice vibrating with all the unleashed emotion of her being, yet with no faltering in it. "If she stays I go."

Stephen Fair, harassed and bewildered, was angry with the relentless anger of a patient man roused at last.

"Go, then," he said sternly, "I'll never turn my mother from my door for any woman's whim."

The stormy red went out of Emily's face, leaving it like a marble wash.

"You mean that!" she said calmly. "Think well. If I go I'll never return."

"I do mean it," said Stephen. "Leave my house if you will — if you hold your marriage vow so lightly. When your senses return you are welcome to come back to me. I will never ask you to."

Without another word Emily turned away. That night she went back to John and Amelia. They, on their part, welcomed her back gladly, believing her to be a wronged and ill-used woman. They hated Stephen Fair with a new and personal rancour. The one thing they could hardly have forgiven Emily would have been the fact of her relenting towards him.

But she did not relent. In her soul she knew that, with all her just grievances, she had been in the wrong, and for that she could not forgive him!

Two years after she had left Stephen Mrs. Fair died, and his widowed sister-in-law went to keep house for him. If he thought of Emily he made no sign. Stephen Fair never broke a word once passed.

Since their separation no greeting or look had ever passed between husband and wife. When they met, as they occasionally did, neither impassive face changed. Emily Fair had buried her love deeply. In her pride and anger she would not let herself remember even where she had dug its grave.

And now Stephen was ill. The strange woman felt a certain pride in her own inflexibility because the fact did not affect her. She told herself that she could not have felt more unconcerned had he been the merest stranger. Nevertheless she waited and watched for John Phillips' homecoming.

At ten o'clock she heard his voice in the kitchen. She leaned out of the bed and pulled open her door. She heard voices below, but could not distinguish the words, so she rose and went noiselessly out into the hall, knelt down by the stair railing and listened. The door of the kitchen was open below her and a narrow shaft of light struck on her white, intent face. She looked like a woman waiting for the decree of doom.

At first John and Amelia talked of trivial matters. Then the latter said abruptly:

"Did you hear how Stephen Fair was?"

"He's dying," was the brief response.

Emily heard Amelia's startled exclamation. She gripped the square rails with her hands until the sharp edges dinted deep into her fingers. John's voice came up to her again, harsh and expressionless:

"He took a bad turn the day before yesterday and has been getting worse ever since. The doctors don't expect him to live till morning."

Amelia began to talk rapidly in low tones. Emily heard nothing further. She got up and went blindly back into her room with such agony tearing at her heartstrings that she dully wondered why she could not shriek aloud.

Stephen — her husband — dying! In the burning anguish of that moment her own soul was as an open book before her. The love she had buried rose from the deeps of her being in an awful, accusing resurrection.

Out of her stupor and pain a purpose formed itself clearly. She must go to Stephen — she must beg and win his forgiveness before it was too late. She dared not go down to John and ask him to take her to her husband. He might refuse. The Phillipses had been known to do even harder things than that. At the best there would be a storm of protest and objection on her brother's and sister's part, and Emily felt that she could not encounter that in her present mood. It would drive her mad.

She lit a lamp and dressed herself noiselessly, but with feverish haste. Then she listened. The house was very still. Amelia and John had gone to bed. She wrapped herself in a heavy woollen shawl hanging in the hall and crept downstairs. With numbed fingers she fumbled at the key of the hall door, turned it and slipped out into the night.

The storm seemed to reach out and clutch her and swallow her up. She went through the garden, where the flowers already were crushed to earth; she crossed the long field beyond, where the rain cut her face like a whip and the wind almost twisted her in its grasp like a broken reed. Somehow or other, more by blind instinct than anything else, she found the path that led through commons and woods and waste valleys to her lost home.

In after years that frenzied walk through the storm and blackness seemed as an unbroken nightmare to Emily Fair's recollection. Often she fell. Once as she did so a jagged, dead limb of fir struck her forehead and cut in it a gash that marked her for life. As she struggled to her feet and found her way again the blood trickled down over her face.

"Oh God, don't let him die before I get to him — don't — don't — don't!" she prayed desperately with more of defiance than entreaty in her voice. Then, realizing this, she cried out in horror. Surely some fearsome punishment would come upon her for her wickedness — she would find her husband lying dead.

When Emily opened the kitchen door of the Fair homestead Almira Sentner cried out in her alarm, who or what was this creature with the white face and wild eyes, with her torn and dripping garments and dishevelled, windwrithen hair and the big drops of blood slowly trickling from her brow?

The next moment she recognized Emily and her face hardened. This woman, Stephen's sister-in-law, had always hated Emily Fair.

"What do you want here?" she said harshly.

"Where is my husband?" asked Emily.

"You can't see him," said Mrs. Sentner defiantly. "The doctors won't allow anyone in the room but those he's used to. Strangers excite him."

46

The insolence and cruelty of her speech fell on unheeding ears. Emily, understanding only that her husband yet lived, turned to the hall door.

"Stand back!" she said in a voice that was little more than a thrilling whisper, but which yet had in it something that cowed Almira Sentner's malice. Sullenly she stood aside and Emily went unhindered up the stairs to the room where the sick man lay.

The two doctors in attendance were there, together with the trained nurse from the city. Emily pushed them aside and fell on her knees by the bed. One of the doctors made a hasty motion as if to draw her back, but the other checked him.

"It doesn't matter now," he said significantly.

Stephen Fair turned his languid, unshorn head on the pillow. His dull, fevered eyes met Emily's. He had not recognized anyone all day, but he knew his wife.

"Emily!" he whispered.

Emily drew his head close to her face and kissed his lips passionately.

"Stephen, I've come back to you. Forgive me — forgive me — say that you forgive me."

"It's all right, my girl," he said feebly.

She buried her face in the pillow beside his with a sob.

In the wan, grey light of the autumn dawn the old doctor came to the bedside and lifted Emily to her feet. She had not stirred the whole night. Now she raised her white face with dumb pleading in her eyes. The doctor glanced at the sleeping form on the bed.

"Your husband will live, Mrs. Fair," he said gently. "I think your coming saved him. His joy turned the ebbing tide in favour of life."

"Thank God!" said Emily.

And for the first time in her life her beautiful voice trembled.

The Girl and The Wild Race

"If Judith would only get married," Mrs. Theodora Whitney was wont to sigh dolorously.

Now, there was no valid reason why Judith ought to get married unless she wanted to. But Judith was twenty-seven and Mrs. Theodora thought it was a terrible disgrace to be an old maid.

"There has never been an old maid in our family so far back as we know of," she lamented. "And to think that there should be one now! It just drags us down to the level of the McGregors. They have always been noted for their old maids."

Judith took all her aunt's lamentations good-naturedly. Sometimes she argued the subject placidly.

"Why are you in such a hurry to be rid of me, Aunt Theo? I'm sure we're very comfortable here together and you know you would miss me terribly if I went away."

"If you took the right one you wouldn't go so very far," said Mrs. Theodora, darkly significant. "And, anyhow, I'd put up with any amount of lonesomeness rather than have an old maid in the family. It's all very fine now, when you're still young enough and good looking, with lots of beaus at your beck and call. But that won't last much longer and if you go on with your dilly-dallying you'll wake up some fine day to find that your time for choosing has gone by. Your mother used to be dreadful proud of your good looks when you was a baby. I told her she needn't be. Nine times out of ten a beauty don't marry as well as an ordinary girl."

"I'm not much set on marrying at all," declared Judith

48

sharply. Any reference to the "right one" always disturbed her placidity. The real root of the trouble was that Mrs. Theodora's "right one" and Judith's "right one" were two different people.

The Ramble Valley young men were very fond of dancing attendance on Judith, even if she were verging on old maidenhood. Her prettiness was undeniable; the Stewarts came to maturity late and at twenty-seven Judith's dower of milky-white flesh, dimpled red lips and shining bronze hair was at its fullest splendor. Besides, she was "jolly," and jollity went a long way in Ramble Valley popularity.

Of all Judith's admirers Eben King alone found favor in Mrs. Theodora's eyes. He owned the adjoining farm, was well off and homely — so homely that Judith declared it made her eyes ache to look at him.

Bruce Marshall, Judith's "right one" was handsome, but Mrs. Theodora looked upon him with sour disapproval. He owned a stony little farm at the remote end of Ramble Valley and was reputed to be fonder of many things than of work. To be sure, Judith had enough capability and energy for two; but Mrs. Theodora detested a lazy man. She ordered Judith not to encourage him and Judith obeyed. Judith generally obeyed her aunt; but, though she renounced Bruce Marshall, she would have nothing to do with Eben King or anybody else and all Mrs. Theodora's grumblings did not mend matters.

The afternoon that Mrs. Tony Mack came in Mrs. Theodora felt more aggrieved than ever. Ellie McGregor had been married the previous week — Ellie, who was the same age as Judith and not half so good looking. Mrs. Theodora had been nagging Judith ever since.

"But I might as well talk to the trees down there in that hollow," she complained to Mrs. Tony. "That girl is so set and contrary minded. She doesn't care a bit for my feelings."

This was not said behind Judith's back. The girl herself was standing at the open door, drinking in all the delicate, evasive beauty of the spring afternoon. The Whitney house crested a bare hill that looked down on misty intervals, feathered with young firs that were golden green in the pale sunlight. The fields were bare and smoking, although the lanes and shadowy places were full of moist snow. Judith's face was aglow with the delight of mere life and she bent out to front the brisk, dancing wind that blew up from the valley, resinous with the odors of firs and damp mosses.

At her aunt's words the glow went out of her face. She listened with her eyes brooding on the hollow and a glowing flame of temper smouldering in them. Judith's long patience was giving way. She had been flicked on the raw too often of late. And now her aunt was confiding her grievances to Mrs. Tony Mack — the most notorious gossip in Ramble Valley or out of it!

"I can't sleep at nights for worrying over what will become of her when I'm gone," went on Mrs. Theodora dismally. "She'll just have to live on alone here — a lonesome, withered-up old maid. And her that might have had her pick, Mrs. Tony, though I do say it as shouldn't. You must feel real thankful to have all your girls married off — especially when none of them was extry good-looking. Some people have all the luck. I'm tired of talking to Judith. Folks'll be saying soon that nobody ever really wanted her, for all her flirting. But she just won't marry."

"I will!"

Judith whirled about on the sun warm door step and came in. Her black eyes were flashing and her round cheeks were crimson.

"Such a temper you never saw!" reported Mrs. Tony afterwards. "Though 'tweren't to be wondered at. Theodora was most awful aggravating."

"I will," repeated Judith stormily. "I'm tired of being nagged day in and day out. I'll marry — and what is more I'll marry the very first man that asks me — that I will, if it is old Widower Delane himself! How does that suit you, Aunt Theodora?"

Mrs. Theodora's mental processes were never slow. She dropped her knitting ball and stooped for it. In that time she had decided what to do. She knew that Judith would stick to her word, Stewart-like, and she must trim her sails to catch this new wind.

"It suits me real well, Judith," she said calmly, "you can marry the first man that asks you and I'll say no word to hinder."

The color went out of Judith's face, leaving it pale as ashes. Her hasty assertion had no sooner been uttered than it was repented of, but she must stand by it now. She went out of the kitchen without another glance at her aunt or the delighted Mrs. Tony and dashed up the stairs to her own little room which looked out over the whole of Ramble Valley. It was warm with the March sunshine and the leafless boughs of the creeper that covered the end of the house were tapping a gay tattoo on the window panes to the music of the wind.

Judith sat down in her little rocker and dropped her pointed chin in her hands. Far down the valley, over the firs on the McGregor hill and the blue mirror of the Cranston pond, Bruce Marshall's little gray house peeped out from a semicircle of white-stemmed birches. She had not seen Bruce since before Christmas. He had been angry at her then because she had refused to let him drive her home from prayer meeting. Since then she had heard a rumor that he was going to see Kitty Leigh at the Upper Valley.

Judith looked sombrely down at the Marshall homestead. She had always loved the quaint, picturesque old place, so different from all the commonplace spick and span new houses of the prosperous valley. Judith had never been able to decide whether she really cared very much for Bruce Marshall or not, but she knew that she loved that rambling, cornery house of his, with the gable festooned with the real ivy that Bruce Marshall's great-grandmother had brought with her from England. Judith thought contrastingly of Eben King's staring, primrose-colored house in all its bare, intrusive grandeur. She gave a little shrug of distaste.

"I wish Bruce knew of this," she thought, flushing even in her solitude at the idea. "Although if it is true that he is going to see Kitty Leigh I don't suppose he'd care. And Aunt Theo will be sure to send word to Eben by hook or crook. Whatever possessed me to say such a mad thing? There goes Mrs. Tony now, all agog to spread such a delectable bit of gossip."

Mrs. Tony had indeed gone, refusing Mrs. Theodora's invitation to stay to tea, so eager was she to tell her story. And Mrs. Theodora, at that very minute, was out in her kitchen yard, giving her instructions to Potter Vane, the twelve year old urchin who cut her wood and did sundry other chores for her.

"Potter," she said, excitedly, "run over to the Kings' and tell Eben to come over here immediately — no matter what he's at. Tell him I want to see him about something of the greatest importance."

Mrs. Theodora thought that this was a master stroke.

"That match is as good as made," she thought triumphantly as she picked up chips to start the tea fire. "If Judith suspects that Eben is here she is quite likely to stay in her room and refuse to come down. But if she does I'll march him upstairs to her door and make him ask her through the keyhole. You can't stump Theodora Whitney."

Alas! Ten minutes later Potter returned with the unwelcome news that Eben was away from home.

"He went to Wexbridge about half an hour ago, his ma said. She said she'd tell him to come right over as soon as he kem home."

Mrs. Theodora had to content herself with this, but she felt troubled. She knew Mrs. Tony Mack's capabilities for spreading news. What if Bruce Marshall should hear it before Eben?

That evening Jacob Plowden's store at Wexbridge was full of men, sitting about on kegs and counters or huddling around the stove, for the March air had grown sharp as the sun lowered in the creamy sky over the Ramble Valley hills. Eben King had a keg in the corner. He was in no hurry to go home for he loved gossip dearly and the Wexbridge stores abounded with it. He had exhausted the news of Peter Stanley's store across the bridge and now he meant to hear what was saying at Plowden's. Bruce Marshall was there, too, buying groceries and being waited on by Nora Plowden, who was by no means averse to the service, although as a rule her father's customers received scanty tolerance at her hands.

"What are the Valley roads like, Marshall?" asked a Wexbridge man, between two squirts of tobacco juice.

"Bad," said Bruce briefly. "Another warm day will finish the sleighing."

"Are they crossing at Malley's Creek yet?" asked Plowden.

"No, Jack Carr got in there day before yesterday. Nearly lost his mare. I came round by the main road," responded Bruce.

The door opened at this point and Tony Mack came in. As soon as he closed the door he doubled up in a fit of chuckles, which lasted until he was purple in the face.

"Is the man crazy?" demanded Plowden, who had never seen lean little Tony visited like this before.

"Crazy nothin'," retorted Tony. "You'll laugh too, when you hear it. Such a joke! Hee-tee-tee-hee-e. Theodora Whitney has been badgering Judith Stewart so much about bein' an old maid that Judith's got mad and vowed she'll marry the first man that asks her. Hee-tee-tee-hee-e-e-e! My old woman was there and heard her. She'll keep her word, too. She ain't old Joshua Stewart's daughter for nothin'. If he said he'd do a thing he did it if it tuck the

53

hair off. If I was a young feller now! Hee-tee-tee-hee-e-e-e!"

Bruce Marshall swung round on one foot. His face was crimson and if looks could kill, Tony Mack would have fallen dead in the middle of his sniggers.

"You needn't mind doing up that parcel for me," he said to Nora. "I'll not wait for it."

On his way to the door Eben King brushed past him. A shout of laughter from the assembled men followed them. The others streamed out in their wake, realizing that a race was afoot. Tony alone remained inside, helpless with chuckling.

Eben King's horse was tied at the door. He had nothing to do but step in and drive off. Bruce had put his mare in at Billy Bender's across the bridge, intending to spend the evening there. He knew that this would handicap him seriously, but he strode down the road with a determined expression on his handsome face. Fifteen minutes later he drove past the store, his gray mare going at a sharp gait. The crowd in front of Plowden's cheered him, their sympathies were with him for King was not popular. Tony had come out and shouted, "Here's luck to you, brother," after which he doubled up with renewed laughter. Such a lark! And he, Tony, had set it afoot! It would be a story to tell for years.

Marshall, with his lips set and his dreamy gray eyes for once glittering with a steely light, urged Lady Jane up the Wexbridge hill. From its top it was five miles to Ramble Valley by the main road. A full mile ahead of him he saw Eben King, getting along through mud and slush, and occasional big slumpy drifts of old snow, as fast as his clean-limbed trotter could carry him. As a rule Eben was exceedingly careful of his horses, but now he was sending Bay Billy along for all that was in him.

For a second Bruce hesitated. Then he turned his mare down the field cut to Malley's Creek. It was taking Lady Jane's life and possibly his own in his hand, but it was his only chance. He could never have overtaken Bay Billy on the main road.

"Do your best, Lady Jane," he muttered, and Lady Jane plunged down the steep hillside, through the glutinous mud of a ploughed field as if she meant to do it.

Beyond the field was a ravine full of firs, through which Malley's Creek ran. To cross it meant a four-mile cut to Ramble Valley. The ice looked black and rotten. To the left was the ragged hole where Jack Carr's mare had struggled for her life. Bruce headed Lady Jane higher up. If a crossing could be made at all it was only between Malley's spring-hole and the old ice road. Lady Jane swerved at the bank and whickered.

"On, old girl," said Bruce, in a tense voice. Unwillingly she advanced, picking her steps with cat-like sagacity. Once her foot went through, Bruce pulled her up with hands that did not tremble. The next moment she was scrambling up the opposite bank. Glancing back, Bruce saw the ice parting in her footprints and the black water gurgling up.

But the race was not yet decided. By crossing the creek he had won no more than an equal chance with Eben King. And the field road before him was much worse than the main road. There was little snow on it and some bad sloughs. But Lady Jane was good for it. For once she should not be spared.

Just as the red ball of the sun touched the wooded hills of the valley, Mrs. Theodora, looking from the cowstable door, saw two sleighs approaching, the horses of which were going at a gallop. One was trundling down the main road, headlong through old drifts and slumpy snow, where a false step might send the horse floundering to the bottom. The other was coming up from the direction of the creek, full tilt through Tony Mack's stump land, where not a vestige of snow coated the huge roots over which the runners bumped.

For a moment Mrs. Theodora stood at a gaze. Then she recognized both drivers. She dropped her milking pail and ran to the house, thinking as she ran. She knew that Judith was alone in the kitchen. If Eben King got there first, well and good, but if Bruce Marshall won the race he must encounter her, Mrs. Theodora.

"He won't propose to Judith as long as I'm round," she panted. "I know him — he's too shy. But Eben won't mind — I'll tip him the wink."

Potter Vane was chopping wood before the door. Mrs. Theodora recognizing in him a further obstacle to Marshall's wooing, caught him unceremoniously by the arm and hauled him, axe and all, over the doorstone and into the kitchen, just as Bruce Marshall and Eben King drove into the yard with not a second to spare between them. There was a woeful cut on Bay Billy's slender fore-leg and the reeking Lady Jane was trembling like a leaf. The staunch little mare had brought her master over that stretch of sticky field road in time, but she was almost exhausted.

Both men sprang from their sleighs and ran to the door. Bruce Marshall won it by foot-room and burst into the kitchen with his rival hot on his heels. Mrs. Theodora stood defiantly in the middle of the room, still grasping the dazed and dismayed Potter. In a corner Judith turned from the window whence she had been watching the finish of the race. She was pale and tense from excitement. In those few gasping moments she had looked on her heart as on an open book; she knew at last that she loved Bruce Marshall and her eyes met his fiery gray ones as he sprang over the threshold.

"Judith, will you marry me?" gasped Bruce, before Eben, who had first looked at Mrs. Theodora and the squirming Potter, had located the girl.

"Yes," said Judith. She burst into hysterical tears as she said it and sat limply down in a chair.

Mrs. Theodora loosed her grip on Potter.

"You can go back to your work," she said dully. She

followed him out and Eben King followed her. On the step she reached behind him and closed the door.

"Trust a King for being too late!" she said bitterly and unjustly.

Eben went home with Bay Billy. Potter gazed after him until Mrs. Theodora ordered him to put Marshall's mare in the stable and rub her down.

"Anyway, Judith won't be an old maid," she comforted herself.

The Promise of Lucy Ellen

Cecily Foster came down the sloping, fir-fringed road from the village at a leisurely pace. Usually she walked with a long, determined stride, but to-day the drowsy, mellowing influence of the Autumn afternoon was strong upon her and filled her with placid content. Without being actively conscious of it, she was satisfied with the existing circumstances of her life. It was half over now. The half of it yet to be lived stretched before her, tranquil, pleasant and uneventful, like the afternoon, filled with unhurried duties and calmly interesting days, Cecily liked the prospect.

When she came to her own lane she paused, folding her hands on the top of the whitewashed gate, while she basked for a moment in the warmth that seemed cupped in the little grassy hollow hedged about with young fir-trees.

Before her lay sere, brooding fields sloping down to a sandy shore, where long foamy ripples were lapping with a murmur that threaded the hushed air like a faint minor melody.

On the crest of the little hill to her right was her home — hers and Lucy Ellen's. The house was an old-fashioned, weather-gray one, low in the eaves, with gables and porches overgrown with vines that had turned to wine-reds and rich bronzes in the October frosts. On three sides it was closed in by tall old spruces, their outer sides bared and grim from long wrestling with the Atlantic winds, but their inner green and feathery. On the fourth side a trim white paling shut in the flower garden before the front door. Cecily could see the beds of purple and scarlet asters, making rich whorls of color under the parlor and sitting-room windows. Lucy Ellen's bed was gayer and larger than Cecily's. Lucy Ellen had always had better luck with flowers.

She could see old Boxer asleep on the front porch step and Lucy Ellen's white cat stretched out on the parlor window-sill. There was no other sign of life about the place. Cecily drew a long, leisurely breath of satisfaction.

"After tea I'll dig up those dahlia roots," she said aloud. "They'd ought to be up. My, how blue and soft that sea is! I never saw such a lovely day. I've been gone longer than I expected. I wonder if Lucy Ellen's been lonesome?"

When Cecily looked back from the misty ocean to the house, she was surprised to see a man coming with a jaunty step down the lane under the gnarled spruces. She looked at him perplexedly. He must be a stranger, for she was sure no man in Oriental walked like that.

"Some agent has been pestering Lucy Ellen, I suppose," she muttered vexedly.

The stranger came on with an airy briskness utterly foreign to Orientalites. Cecily opened the gate and went through. They met under the amber-tinted sugar maple in the heart of the hollow. As he passed, the man lifted his hat and bowed with an ingratiating smile.

He was about forty-five, well, although somewhat loudly dressed, and with an air of self-satisfied prosperity pervading his whole personality. He had a heavy gold watch chain and a large seal ring on the hand that lifted his hat. He was bald, with a high, Shaksperian forehead and a halo of sandy curls. His face was ruddy and weak, but good-natured: his eyes were large and blue, and he had a little straw-colored moustache, with a juvenile twist and curl in it.

Cecily did not recognize him, yet there was something vaguely familiar about him. She walked rapidly up to the house. In the sitting-room she found Lucy Ellen peering out between the muslin window curtains. When the latter

59

turned there was an air of repressed excitement about her.

"Who was that man, Lucy Ellen?" Cecily asked.

To Cecily's amazement, Lucy Ellen blushed — a warm, Spring-like flood of color that rolled over her delicate little face like a miracle of rejuvenescence.

"Didn't you know him? That was Cromwell Biron," she simpered. Although Lucy Ellen was forty and, in most respects, sensible, she could not help simpering upon occasion.

"Cromwell Biron," repeated Cecily, in an emotionless voice. She took off her bonnet mechanically, brushed the dust from its ribbons and bows and went to put it carefully away in its white box in the spare bedroom. She felt as if she had had a severe shock, and she dared not ask anything more just then. Lucy Ellen's blush had frightened her. It seemed to open up dizzying possibilities of change.

"But she promised — she promised," said Cecily fiercely, under her breath.

While Cecily was changing her dress, Lucy Ellen was getting the tea ready in the little kitchen. Now and then she broke out into singing, but always checked herself guiltily. Cecily heard her and set her firm mouth a little firmer.

"If a man had jilted me twenty years ago, I wouldn't be so overwhelmingly glad to see him when he came back — especially if he had got fat and bald-headed," she added, her face involuntarily twitching into a smile. Cecily, in spite of her serious expression and intense way of looking at life, had an irrepressible sense of humor.

Tea that evening was not the pleasant meal it usually was. The two women were wont to talk animatedly to each other, and Cecily had many things to tell Lucy Ellen. She did not tell them. Neither did Lucy Ellen ask any questions, her ill-concealed excitement hanging around her like a festal garment.

Cecily's heart was on fire with alarm and jealousy. She smiled a little cruelly as she buttered and ate her toast.

"And so that was Cromwell Biron," she said with studied

carelessness. "I thought there was something familiar about him. When did he come home?"

"He got to Oriental yesterday," fluttered back Lucy Ellen. "He's going to be home for two months. We—we had such an interesting talk this afternoon. He—he's as full of jokes as ever. I wished you'd been here."

This was a fib. Cecily knew it.

"I don't, then," she said contemptuously. "You know I never had much use for Cromwell Biron. I think he had a face of his own to come down here to see you uninvited, after the way he treated you."

Lucy Ellen blushed scorchingly and was miserably silent.

"He's changed terrible in his looks," went on Cecily relentlessly. "How bald he's got — and fat! To think of the spruce Cromwell Biron got to be bald and fat! To be sure, he still has the same sheepish expression. Will you pass me the currant jell, Lucy Ellen?"

"I don't think he's so very fat," she said resentfully, when Cecily had left the table. "And I don't care if he is."

Twenty years before this, Biron had jilted Lucy Ellen Foster. She was the prettiest girl in Oriental then, but the new school teacher over at the Crossways was prettier, with a dash of piquancy, which Lucy Ellen lacked, into the bargain. Cromwell and the school teacher had run away and been married, and Lucy Ellen was left to pick up the tattered shreds of her poor romance as best she could.

She never had another lover. She told herself that she would always be faithful to the one love of her life. This sounded romantic, and she found a certain comfort in it.

She had been brought up by her uncle and aunt. When they died she and her cousin, Cecily Foster, found themselves, except for each other, alone in the world.

Cecily loved Lucy Ellen as a sister. But she believed that Lucy Ellen would yet marry, and her heart sank at the prospect of being left without a soul to love and care for.

It was Lucy Ellen that had first proposed their mutual promise, but Cecily had grasped at it eagerly. The two women, verging on decisive old maidenhood, solemnly promised each other that they would never marry, and would always live together. From that time Cecily's mind had been at ease. In her eyes a promise was a sacred thing.

The next evening at prayer-meeting Cromwell Biron received quite an ovation from old friends and neighbors. Cromwell had been a favorite in his boyhood. He had now the additional glamour of novelty and reputed wealth.

He was beaming and expansive. He went into the choir to help sing. Lucy Ellen sat beside him, and they sang from the same book. Two red spots burned on her thin cheeks, and she had a cluster of lavender chrysanthemums pinned on her jacket. She looked almost girlish, and Cromwell Biron gazed at her with sidelong admiration, while Cecily watched them both fiercely from her pew. She knew that Cromwell Biron had come home, wooing his old love.

"But he sha'n't get her," Cecily whispered into her hymnbook. Somehow it was a comfort to articulate the words, "She promised."

On the church steps Cromwell offered his arm to Lucy Ellen with a flourish. She took it shyly, and they started down the road in the crisp Autumn moonlight. For the first time in ten years Cecily walked home from prayer-meeting alone. She went up-stairs and flung herself on her bed, reckless for once, of her second best hat and gown.

Lucy Ellen did not venture to ask Cromwell in. She was too much in awe of Cecily for that. But she loitered with him at the gate until the grandfather's clock in the hall struck eleven. Then Cromwell went away, whistling gaily, with Lucy Ellen's chrysanthemum in his buttonhole, and Lucy Ellen went in and cried half the night. But Cecily did not cry. She lay savagely awake until morning.

"Cromwell Biron is courting you again," she said bluntly to Lucy Ellen at the breakfast table.

Lucy Ellen blushed nervously.

"Oh, nonsense, Cecily," she protested with a simper.

"It isn't nonsense," said Cecily calmly. "He is. There is no fool like an old fool, and Cromwell Biron never had much sense. The presumption of him!"

Lucy Ellen's hands trembled as she put her teacup down.

"He's not so very old," she said faintly, "and everybody but you likes him — and he's well-to-do. I don't see that there's any presumption."

"Maybe not — if you look at it so. You're very forgiving, Lucy Ellen. You've forgotten how he treated you once."

"No—o—o, I haven't," faltered Lucy Ellen.

"Anyway," said Cecily coldly, "you shouldn't encourage his attentions, Lucy Ellen; you know you couldn't marry him even if he asked you. You promised."

All the fitful color went out of Lucy Ellen's face. Under Cecily's pitiless eyes she wilted and drooped.

"I know," she said deprecatingly, "I haven't forgotten. You are talking nonsense, Cecily. I like to see Cromwell, and he likes to see me because I'm almost the only one of his old set that is left. He feels lonesome in Oriental now."

Lucy Ellen lifted her fawn-colored little head more erectly at the last of her protest. She had saved her self-respect.

In the month that followed Cromwell Biron pressed his suit persistently, unintimidated by Cecily's antagonism. October drifted into November and the chill, drear days came. To Cecily the whole outer world seemed the dismal reflex of her pain-bitten heart. Yet she constantly laughed at herself, too, and her laughter was real if bitter.

One evening she came home late from a neighbor's. Cromwell Biron passed her in the hollow under the bare boughs of the maple that were outlined against the silvery moonlit sky.

When Cecily went into the house, Lucy Ellen opened the parlor door. She was very pale, but her eyes burned in her face and her hands were clasped before her.

"I wish you'd come in here for a few minutes, Cecily," she said feverishly.

Cecily followed silently into the room.

"Cecily," she said faintly, "Cromwell was here to-night. He asked me to marry him. I told him to come to-morrow night for his answer."

She paused and looked imploringly at Cecily. Cecily did not speak. She stood tall and unrelenting by the table. The rigidity of her face and figure smote Lucy Ellen like a blow. She threw out her bleached little hands and spoke with a sudden passion utterly foreign to her.

"Cecily, I want to marry him. I—I—love him. I always have. I never thought of this when I promised. Oh, Cecily, you'll let me off my promise, won't you?"

"No," said Cecily. It was all she said. Lucy Ellen's hands fell to her sides, and the light went out of her face.

"You won't?" she said hopelessly.

Cecily went out. At the door she turned.

"When John Edwards asked me to marry him six years ago, I said no for your sake. To my mind a promise is a promise. But you were always weak and romantic, Lucy Ellen."

Lucy Ellen made no response. She stood limply on the hearth-rug like a faded blossom bitten by frost.

After Cromwell Biron had gone away the next evening, with all his brisk jauntiness shorn from him for the time, Lucy Ellen went up to Cecily's room. She stood for a moment in the narrow doorway, with the lamplight striking upward with a gruesome effect on her wan face.

"I've sent him away," she said lifelessly. "I've kept my promise, Cecily."

There was silence for a moment. Cecily did not know what to say. Suddenly Lucy Ellen burst out bitterly.

"I wish I was dead!"

Then she turned swiftly and ran across the hall to her own room. Cecily gave a little moan of pain. This was her reward for all the love she had lavished on Lucy Ellen.

"Anyway, it is all over," she said, looking dourly into the moonlit boughs of the firs; "Lucy Ellen'll get over it.

When Cromwell is gone she'll forget all about him. I'm not going to fret. She promised, and she wanted the promise first."

During the next fortnight tragedy held grim sway in the little weather-gray house among the firs — a tragedy tempered with grim comedy for Cecily, who, amid all her agony, could not help being amused at Lucy Ellen's romantic way of sorrowing.

Lucy Ellen did her mornings' work listlessly and drooped through the afternoons. Cecily would have felt it as a relief if Lucy Ellen had upbraided her, but after her outburst on the night she sent Cromwell away, Lucy Ellen never uttered a word of reproach or complaint.

One evening Cecily made a neighborly call in the village. Cromwell Biron happened to be there and gallantly insisted upon seeing her home.

She understood from Cromwell's unaltered manner that Lucy Ellen had not told him why she had refused him. She felt a sudden admiration for her cousin.

When they reached the house Cromwell halted suddenly in the banner of light that streamed from the sitting-room window. They saw Lucy Ellen sitting alone before the fire, her arms folded on the table, and her head bowed on them. Her white cat sat unnoticed at the table beside her. Cecily gave a gasp of surrender.

"You'd better come in," she said, harshly. "Lucy Ellen looks lonesome."

Cromwell muttered sheepishly, "I'm afraid I wouldn't be company for her. Lucy Ellen doesn't like me much—"

"Oh, doesn't she!" said Cecily, bitterly. "She likes you better than she likes me for all I've—but it's no matter. It's been all my fault — she'll explain. Tell her I said she could. Come in, I say."

She caught the still reluctant Cromwell by the arm and fairly dragged him over the geranium beds and through the front door. She opened the sitting-room door and pushed him in. Lucy Ellen rose in amazement. Over

Cromwell's bald head loomed Cecily's dark face, tragic and determined.

"Here's your beau, Lucy Ellen," she said, "and I give you back your promise."

She shut the door upon the sudden illumination of Lucy Ellen's face and went up-stairs with the tears rolling down her cheeks.

"It's my turn to wish I was dead," she muttered. Then she laughed hysterically.

"That goose of a Cromwell! How queer he did look standing there, frightened to death of Lucy Ellen. Poor little Lucy Ellen! Well, I hope he'll be good to her."

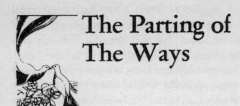

The Parting of The Ways

Mrs. Longworth crossed the hotel piazza, descended the steps, and walked out of sight down the shore road with all the grace of motion that lent distinction to her slightest movement. Her eyes were very bright, and an unusual flush stained the pallor of her cheek. Two men who were lounging in one corner of the hotel piazza looked admiringly after her.

"She is a beautiful woman," said one.

"Wasn't there some talk about Mrs. Longworth and Cunningham last winter?" asked the other.

"Yes. They were much together. Still, there may have been nothing wrong. She was old Judge Carmody's daughter, you know. Longworth got Carmody under his thumb in money matters and put the screws on. They say he made Carmody's daughter the price of the old man's redemption. The girl herself was a mere child. I shall never forget her face on her wedding day. But she's been plucky since then, I must say. If she has suffered, she hasn't shown it. I don't suppose Longworth ever ill-treats her. He isn't that sort. He's simply a grovelling cad — that's all. Nobody would sympathise much with the poor devil if his wife did run off with Cunningham."

Meanwhile, Beatrice Longworth walked quickly down the shore road, her white skirt brushing over the crisp golden grasses by the way. In a sunny hollow among the sandhills she came upon Stephen Gordon, sprawled out luxuriously in the warm, sea-smelling grasses. The youth sprang to his feet at sight of her, and his big brown eyes kindled to a glow.

Mrs. Longworth smiled to him. They had been great friends all summer. He was a lanky, overgrown lad of fifteen or sixteen, odd and shy and dreamy, scarcely possessing a speaking acquaintance with others at the hotel. But he and Mrs. Longworth had been congenial from their first meeting. In many ways, he was far older than his years, but there was a certain inerradicable boyishness about him to which her heart warmed.

"You are the very person I was just going in search of. I've news to tell. Sit down."

He spoke eagerly, patting the big gray boulder beside him with his slim, brown hand. For a moment Beatrice hesitated. She wanted to be alone just then. But his clever, homely face was so appealing that she yielded and sat down.

Stephen flung himself down again contentedly in the grasses at her feet, pillowing his chin in his palms and looking up at her, adoringly.

"You are so beautiful, dear lady. I love to look at you. Will you tilt that hat a little more over the left eye-brow? Yes—so—some day I shall paint you."

His tone and manner were all simplicity.

"When you are a great artist," said Beatrice, indulgently.

He nodded.

"Yes, I mean to be that. I've told you all my dreams, you know. Now for my news. I'm going away to-morrow. I had a telegram from father to-day."

He drew the message from his pocket and flourished it up at her.

"I'm to join him in Europe at once. He is in Rome. Think of it — in Rome! I'm to go on with my art studies there. And I leave to-morrow."

"I'm glad — and I'm sorry — and you know which is which," said Beatrice, patting the shaggy brown head. "I shall miss you dreadfully, Stephen."

"We *have* been splendid chums, haven't we?" he said, eagerly.

Suddenly his face changed. He crept nearer to her, and

bowed his head until his lips almost touched the hem of her dress.

"I'm glad you came down to-day," he went on in a low, diffident voice. "I want to tell you something, and I can tell it better here. I couldn't go away without thanking you. I'll make a mess of it — I can never explain things. But you've been so much to me — you mean so much to me. You've made me believe in things I never believed in before. You—you—I know now that there *is* such a thing as a good woman, a woman who could make a man better, just because he breathed the same air with her."

He paused for a moment; then went on in a still lower tone:

"It's hard when a fellow can't speak of his mother because he can't say anything good of her, isn't it? My mother wasn't a good woman. When I was eight years old she went away with a scoundrel. It broke father's heart. Nobody thought I understood, I was such a little fellow. But I did. I heard them talking. I knew she had brought shame and disgrace on herself and us. And I had loved her so! Then, somehow, as I grew up, it was my misfortune that all the women I had to do with were mean and base. They were hirelings, and I hated and feared them. There was an aunt of mine — she tried to be good to me in her way. But she told me a lie, and I never cared for her after I found it out. And then, father — we loved each other and were good chums. But he didn't believe in much either. He was bitter, you know. He said all women were alike. I grew up with that notion. I didn't care much for anything — nothing seemed worth while. Then I came here and met you."

He paused again. Beatrice had listened with a gray look on her face. It would have startled him had he glanced up, but he did not, and after a moment's silence the halting boyish voice went on:

"You have changed everything for me. I was nothing but a clod before. You are not the mother of my body, but you are of my soul. It was born of you. I shall always love and reverence you for it. You will always be my ideal. If I ever do anything worth while it will be because of you. In everything I shall ever attempt I shall try to do it as if you were to pass judgment upon it. You will be a lifelong inspiration to me. Oh, I am bungling this! I can't tell you what I feel — you are so pure, so good, so noble! I shall reverence all women for your sake henceforth."

"And if," said Beatrice, in a very low voice, "if I were false to your ideal of me — if I were to do anything that would destroy your faith in me — something weak or wicked—"

"But you couldn't," he interrupted, flinging up his head and looking at her with his great dog-like eyes, "you couldn't!"

"But if I could?" she persisted, gently, "and if I did — what then?"

"I should hate you," he said, passionately. "You would be worse than a murderess. You would kill every good impulse and belief in me. I would never trust anything or anybody again — but there," he added, his voice once more growing tender, "you will never fail me, I feel sure of that."

"Thank you," said Beatrice, almost in a whisper. "Thank you," she repeated, after a moment. She stood up and held out her hand. "I think I must go now. Good-bye, dear laddie. Write to me from Rome. I shall always be glad to hear from you wherever you are. And—and—I shall always try to live up to your ideal of me, Stephen."

He sprang to his feet and took her hand, lifting it to his lips with boyish reverence. "I know that," he said, slowly. "Good-bye, my sweet lady."

When Mrs. Longworth found herself in her room again, she unlocked her desk and took out a letter. It was addressed to Mr. Maurice Cunningham. She slowly tore it twice across, laid the fragments on a tray, and touched them with a lighted match. As they blazed up one line came out in writhing redness across the page: "I will go away with you as you ask." Then it crumbled into gray ashes.

She drew a long breath and hid her face in her hands.

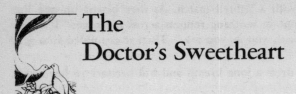

The Doctor's Sweetheart

Just because I am an old woman outwardly it doesn't follow that I am one inwardly. Hearts don't grow old — or shouldn't. Mine hasn't, I am thankful to say. It bounded like a girl's with delight when I saw Doctor John and Marcella Barry drive past this afternoon. If the doctor had been my own son I couldn't have felt more real pleasure in his happiness. I'm only an old lady who can do little but sit by her window and knit, but eyes were made for seeing, and I use mine for that purpose. When I see the good and beautiful things — and a body need never look for the other kind, you know — the things God planned from the beginning and brought about in spite of the counter plans and schemes of men, I feel such a deep joy that I'm glad, even at seventy-five, to be alive in a world where such things come to pass. And if ever God meant and made two people for each other, those people were Doctor John and Marcella Barry; and that is what I always tell folk who come here commenting on the difference in their ages. "Old enough to be her father," sniffed Mrs. Riddell to me the other day. I didn't say anything to Mrs. Riddell. I just looked at her. I presume my face expressed what I felt pretty clearly. How any woman can live for sixty years in the world, as Mrs. Riddell has, a wife and mother at that, and not get some realization of the beauty and general satisfactoriness of a real and abiding love, is something I cannot understand and never shall be able to.

Nobody in Bridgeport believed that Marcella would ever come back, except Doctor John and me — not even her Aunt Sara. I've heard people laugh at me when I said

I knew she would; but nobody minds being laughed at when she is sure of a thing and I was sure that Marcella Barry would come back as that the sun rose and set. I hadn't lived beside her for eight years to know so little about her as to doubt her. Neither had Doctor John.

Marcella was only eight years old when she came to live in Bridgeport. Her father, Chester Barry, had just died. Her mother, who was a sister of Miss Sara Bryant, my next door neighbor, had been dead for four years. Marcella's father left her to the guardianship of his brother, Richard Barry; but Miss Sara pleaded so hard to have the little girl that the Barrys consented to let Marcella live with her aunt until she was sixteen. Then, they said, she would have to go back to them, to be properly educated and take the place of her father's daughter in *his* world. For, of course, it is a fact that Miss Sara Bryant's world was and is a very different one from Chester Barry's world. As to which side the difference favors, that isn't for me to say. It all depends on your standard of what is really worth while, you know.

So Marcella came to live with us in Bridgeport. I say "us" advisedly. She slept and ate in her aunt's house, but every house in the village was a home to her; for, with all our little disagreements and diverse opinions, we are really all one big family, and everybody feels an interest in and a good working affection for everybody else. Besides, Marcella was one of those children whom everybody loves at sight, and keeps on loving. One long, steady gaze from those big grayish-blue black-lashed eyes of hers went right into your heart and stayed there.

She was a pretty child and as good as she was pretty. It was the right sort of goodness, too, with just enough spice of original sin in it to keep it from spoiling by reason of over-sweetness. She was a frank, loyal, brave little thing, even at eight, and wouldn't have said or done a mean or false thing to save her life.

She and I were right good friends from the beginning. She loved me and she loved her Aunt Sara; but from the very first her best and deepest affection went out to Doctor John Haven, who lived in the big brick house on the other side of Miss Sara's.

Doctor John was a Bridgeport boy, and when he got through college he came right home and settled down here, with his widowed mother. The Bridgeport girls were fluttered, for eligible young men were scarce in our village; there was considerable setting of caps, I must say that, although I despise ill-natured gossip; but neither the caps nor the wearers thereof seemed to make any impression on Doctor John. Mrs. Riddell said that he was a born old bachelor; I suppose she based her opinion on the fact that Doctor John was always a quiet, bookish fellow, who didn't care a button for society, and had never been guilty of a flirtation in his life. I knew Doctor John's heart far better than Martha Riddell could know anybody's; and I knew there was nothing of the old bachelor in his nature. He just had to wait for the right woman, that was all, not being able to content himself with less as some men can and do. If she never came Doctor John would never marry; but he wouldn't be an old bachelor for all that.

He was thirty when Marcella came to Bridgeport — a tall, broad-shouldered man with a mane of thick brown curls and level, dark hazel eyes. He walked with a little stoop, his hands clasped behind him; and he had the sweetest, deepest voice. Spoken music, if ever a voice was. He was kind and brave and gentle, but a little distant and reserved with most people. Everybody in Bridgeport liked him, but only a very few ever passed the inner gates of his confidence or were admitted to any share in his real life. I am proud to say I was one; I think it is something for an old woman to boast of.

Doctor John was always fond of children, and they of him. It was natural that he and little Marcella should take to each other. He had the most to do with bringing her up, for Miss Sara consulted him in everything. Marcella was not hard to manage for the most part; but she had a will of her own, and when she did set it up in opposition to the powers that were, nobody but the doctor could influence her at all; she never resisted him or disobeyed his wishes.

Marcella was one of those girls who develop early. I suppose her constant association with us elderly folks had something to do with it, too. But, at fifteen, she was a woman, loving, beautiful, and spirited.

And Doctor John loved her — loved the woman, not the child. I knew it before he did — but not, as I think, before Marcella did, for those young, straight-gazing eyes of hers were wonderfully quick to read into other people's hearts. I watched them together and saw the love growing between them, like a strong, fair, perfect flower, whose fragrance was to endure for eternity. Miss Sara saw it, too, and was half-pleased and half-worried; even Miss Sara thought the Doctor too old for Marcella; and besides, there were the Barrys to be reckoned with. Those Barrys were the nightmare dread of poor Miss Sara's life.

The time came when Doctor John's eyes were opened. He looked into his own heart and read there what life had written for him. As he told me long afterwards, it came to him with a shock that left him white-lipped. But he was a brave, sensible fellow and he looked the matter squarely in the face. First of all, he put away to one side all that the world might say; the thing concerned solely him and Marcella, and the world had nothing to do with it. That disposed of, he asked himself soberly if he had a right to try to win Marcella's love. He decided that he had not; it would be taking an unfair advantage of her youth and in-experience. He knew that she must soon go to her father's people — she must not go bound by any ties of his making. Doctor John, for Marcella's sake, gave the decision against his own heart.

So much did Doctor John tell me, his old friend and confidant. I said nothing and gave no advice, not having lived seventy-five years for nothing. I knew that Doctor John's decision was manly and right and fair; but I also knew it was all nullified by the fact that Marcella already loved him.

So much I knew; the rest I was left to suppose. The Doctor and Marcella told me much, but there were some things too sacred to be told, even to me. So that to this day I don't know how the doctor found out that Marcella loved him. All I know is that one day, just a month before her sixteenth birthday, the two came hand in hand to Miss Sara and me, as we sat on Miss Sara's veranda in the twilight, and told us simply that they had plighted their troth to each other.

I looked at them standing there with that wonderful sunrise of life and love on their faces — the doctor, tall and serious, with a sprinkle of silver in his brown hair and the smile of a happy man on his lips — Marcella, such a slip of a girl, with her black hair in a long braid and her lovely face all dewed over with tears and sunned over with smiles — I, an old woman, looked at them and thanked the good God for them and their delight.

Miss Sara laughed and cried and kissed — and forboded what the Barrys would do. Her forebodings proved only too true. When the doctor wrote to Richard Barry, Marcella's guardian, asking his consent to their engagement, Richard Barry promptly made trouble — the very worst kind of trouble. He descended on Bridgeport and completely overwhelmed poor Miss Sara in his wrath. He laughed at the idea of countenancing an engagement between a child like Marcella and an obscure country doctor. And he carried Marcella off with him!

She had to go, of course. He was her legal guardian and he would listen to no pleadings. He didn't know anything about Marcella's character, and he thought that a new life out in the great world would soon blot out her fancy.

After the first outburst of tears and prayers Marcella took it very calmly, as far as outward eye could see. She was as cool and dignified and stately as a young queen. On the night before she went away she came over to say good-bye to me. She did not even shed any tears, but the look in her eyes told of bitter hurt. "It is goodbye for five years, Miss Tranquil," she said steadily. "When I am twenty-one I will come back. That is the only promise I can make. They will not let me write to John or Aunt Sara and I will do nothing underhanded. But I will not forget and I will come back."

Richard Barry would not even let her see Doctor John alone again. She had to bid him good-bye beneath the cold, contemptuous eyes of the man of the world. So there was just a hand-clasp and one long deep look between them that was tenderer than any kiss and more eloquent than any words.

"I will come back when I am twenty-one," said Marcella. And I saw Richard Barry smile.

So Marcella went away and in all Bridgeport there were only two people who believed she would ever return. There is no keeping a secret in Bridgeport, and everybody knew all about the love affair between Marcella and the doctor and about the promise she had made. Everybody sympathized with the doctor because everybody believed he had lost his sweetheart.

"For of course she'll never come back," said Mrs. Riddell to me. "She's only a child and she'll soon forget him. She's to be sent to school and taken abroad and between times she'll live with the Richard Barrys; and they move, as everyone knows, in the very highest and gayest circles. I'm sorry for the doctor, though. A man of his age doesn't get over a thing like that in a hurry and he was perfectly silly over Marcella. But it really serves him right for falling in love with a child."

There are times when Martha Riddell gets on my nerves. She's a good-hearted woman, and she means well; but she rasps — rasps terribly.

Even Miss Sara exasperated me. But then she had her excuse. The child she loved as her own had been torn from her and it almost broke her heart. But even so, I thought she ought to have had a little more faith in Marcella.

"Oh, no, she'll never come back," sobbed Miss Sara. "Yes, I know she promised. But they'll wean her away from me. She'll have such a gay, splendid life she'll not want to come back. Five years is a lifetime at her age. No, don't try to comfort me, Miss Tranquil, because I *won't* be comforted!"

When a person has made up her mind to be miserable you just have to *let* her be miserable.

I almost dreaded to see Doctor John for fear he would be in despair, too, without any confidence in Marcella. But when he came I saw I needn't have worried. The light had all gone out of his eyes, but there was a calm, steady patience in them.

"She will come back to me, Miss Tranquil," he said. "I know what people are saying, but that does not trouble me. They do not know Marcella as I do. She promised and she will keep her word — keep it joyously and gladly, too. If I did not know that I would not wish its fulfilment. When she is free she will turn her back on that brilliant world and all it offers her and come back to me. My part is to wait and believe."

So Doctor John waited and believed. After a little while the excitement died away and people forgot Marcella. We never heard from or about her, except a paragraph now and then in the society columns of the city paper the doctor took. We knew she was sent to school for three years; then the Barrys took her abroad. She was presented at court. When the doctor read this — he was with me at the time — he put his hand over his eyes and sat very silent for a long time. I wondered if at last some momentary doubt had crept into his mind — if he did not fear that Marcella must have forgotten him. The paper told of her triumph and her beauty and hinted at a titled match. Was it probable or even possible that she would be faithful to him after all this?

The doctor must have guessed my thoughts, for at last he looked up with a smile.

"She will come back," was all he said. But I saw that the doubt, if doubt it were, had gone. I watched him as he went away, that tall, gentle, kindly-eyed man, and I prayed that his trust might not be misplaced; for if it should be it would break his heart.

Five years seems a long time in looking forward. But they pass quickly. One day I remembered that it was Marcella's twenty-first birthday. Only one other person thought of it. Even Miss Sara did not. Miss Sara remembered Marcella only as a child that had been loved and lost. Nobody else in Bridgeport thought about her at all. The doctor came in that evening. He had a rose in his buttonhole and he walked with a step as light as a boy's.

"She is free to-day," he said. "We shall soon have her again, Miss Tranquil."

"Do you think she will be the same?" I said.

I don't know what made me say it. I hate to be one of those people who throw cold water on other peoples' hopes. But it slipped out before I thought. I suppose the doubt had been vaguely troubling me always, under all my faith in Marcella, and now made itself felt in spite of me.

But the doctor only laughed.

"How could she be changed?" he said. "Some women might be — most women would be — but not Marcella. Dear Miss Tranquil, don't spoil your beautiful record of confidence by doubting her now. We shall have her again soon — how soon I don't know, for I don't even know where she is, whether in the old world or the new — but just as soon as she can come to us."

We said nothing more — neither of us. But every day the light in the doctor's eyes grew brighter and deeper and tenderer. He never spoke of Marcella, but I knew she was in his thoughts every moment. He was much calmer than I was. I trembled when the postman knocked, jumped when the gate latch clicked, and fairly had a cold chill if I saw a telegraph boy running down the street.

One evening, a fortnight later, I went over to see Miss Sara. She was out somewhere, so I sat down in her little sitting room to wait for her. Presently the doctor came in and we sat in the soft twilight, talking a little now and then, but silent when we wanted to be, as becomes real friendship. It was such a beautiful evening. Outside in Miss Sara's garden the roses were white and red, and sweet with dew; the honeysuckle at the window sent in delicious breaths now and again; a few sleepy birds were twittering; between the trees the sky was all pink and silvery blue and there was an evening star over the elm in my front yard. We heard somebody come through the door and down the hall. I turned, expecting to see Miss Sara — and I saw Marcella! She was standing in the doorway, tall and beautiful, with a ray of sunset light falling athwart her black hair under her travelling hat. She was looking past me at Doctor John and in her splendid eyes was the look of the exile who had come home to her own.

"Marcella!" said the doctor.

I went out by the dining-room door and shut it behind me, leaving them alone together.

The wedding is to be next month. Miss Sara is beside herself with delight. The excitement has been really terrible, and the way people have talked and wondered and exclaimed has almost worn my patience clean out. I've snubbed more persons in the last ten days than I ever did in all my life before.

Nothing of this worries Doctor John or Marcella. They are too happy to care for gossip or outside curiosity. The Barrys are not coming to the wedding, I understand. They refuse to forgive Marcella or countenance her folly, as they call it, in any way. Folly! When I see those two together and realize what they mean to each other I have some humble, reverent idea of what true wisdom is.

By Grace of
Julius Caesar

Melissa sent word on Monday evening that she thought we had better go round with the subscription list for cushioning the church pews on Tuesday. I sent back word that I thought we had better go on Thursday. I had no particular objection to Tuesday, but Melissa is rather fond of settling things without consulting anyone else, and I don't believe in always letting her have her own way. Melissa is my cousin and we have always been good friends, and I am really very fond of her; but there's no sense in lying down and letting yourself be walked over. We finally compromised on Wednesday.

I always have a feeling of dread when I hear of any new church-project for which money will be needed, because I know perfectly well that Melissa and I will be sent round to collect for it. People say we seem to be able to get more than anybody else; and they appear to think that because Melissa is an unencumbered old maid, and I am an unencumbered widow, we can spare the time without any inconvenience to ourselves. Well, we have been canvassing for building funds, and socials, and suppers for years, but it is needed now; at least, I have had enough of it, and I should think Melissa has, too.

We started out bright and early on Wednesday morning, for Jersey Cove is a big place and we knew we should need the whole day. We had to walk because neither of us owned a horse, and anyway it's more nuisance getting out to open and shut gates than it is worth while. It was a lovely day then, though promising to be hot, and our hearts were as light as could be expected, considering the disagreeable expedition we were on.

I was waiting at my gate for Melissa when she came, and she looked me over with wonder and disapproval. I could see she thought I was a fool to dress up in my second best flowered muslin and my very best hat with the pale pink roses in it to walk about in the heat and dust; but I wasn't. All my experience in canvassing goes to show that the better dressed and better looking you are the more money you'll get — that is, when it's the men you have to tackle, as in this case. If it had been the women, however, I would have put on the oldest and ugliest things, consistent with decency, I had. This was what Melissa had done, as it was, and she did look fearfully prim and dowdy, except for her front hair, which was as soft and fluffy and elaborate as usual. I never could understand how Melissa always got it arranged so beautifully.

Nothing particular happened the first part of the day. Some few growled and wouldn't subscribe anything, but on the whole we did pretty well. If it had been a missionary subscription we should have fared worse; but when it was something touching their own comfort, like cushioning the pews, they came down handsomely. We reached Daniel Wilson's by noon, and had to have dinner there. We didn't eat much, although we were hungry enough — Mary Wilson's cooking is a by-word in Jersey Cove. No wonder Daniel is dyspeptic; but dyspeptic or not, he gave us a big subscription for our cushions and told us we looked younger than ever. Daniel is always very complimentary, and they say Mary is jealous.

When we left the Wilson's Melissa said, with an air of a woman nerving herself to a disagreeable duty:

"I suppose we might as well go to Isaac Appleby's now and get it over."

I agreed with her. I had been dreading that call all day. It isn't a very pleasant thing to go to a man you have recently refused to marry and ask him for money; and Melissa and I were both in that predicament.

Isaac was a well-to-do old bachelor who had never had any notion of getting married until his sister died in the winter. And then, as soon as the spring planting was over, he began to look round for a wife. He came to me first and I said "No" good and hard. I liked Isaac well enough; but I was snug and comfortable, and didn't feel like pulling up my roots and moving into another lot; besides, Isaac's courting seemed to me a shade too business-like. I can't get along without a little romance; it's my nature.

Isaac was disappointed and said so, but intimated that it wasn't crushing and that the next best would do very well. The next best was Melissa, and he proposed to her after the decent interval of a fortnight. Melissa also refused him. I admit I was surprised at this, for I knew Melissa was rather anxious to marry; but she has always been down on Isaac Appleby, from principle, because of a family feud on her mother's side; besides, an old beau of hers, a widower at Kingsbridge, was just beginning to take notice again, and I suspected Melissa had hopes concerning him. Finally, I imagine Melissa did not fancy being second choice.

Whatever her reasons were, she refused poor Isaac, and that finished his matrimonial prospects as far as Jersey Cove was concerned, for there wasn't another eligible woman in it — that is, for a man of Isaac's age. I was the only widow, and the other old maids besides Melissa were all hopelessly old-maiden.

This was all three months ago, and Isaac had been keeping house for himself ever since. Nobody knew much about how he got along, for the Appleby house is half a mile from anywhere, down near the shore at the end of a long lane — the lonesomest place, as I did not fail to remember when I was considering Isaac's offer.

"I heard Jarvis Aldrich say Isaac had got a dog lately," said Melissa, when we finally came in sight of the house — a handsome new one, by the way, put up only ten years ago. "Jarvis said it was an imported breed. I do hope it isn't cross."

I have a mortal horror of dogs, and I followed Melissa into the big farmyard with fear and trembling. We were halfway across the yard when Melissa shrieked:

"Anne, there's the dog!"

There was the dog; and the trouble was that he didn't stay there, but came right down the slope at a steady, business-like trot. He was a bull-dog and big enough to bite a body clean in two, and he was the ugliest thing in dogs I had ever seen.

Melissa and I both lost our heads. We screamed, dropped our parasols, and ran instinctively to the only refuge that was in sight — a ladder leaning against the old Appleby house. I am forty-five and something more than plump, so that climbing ladders is not my favorite form of exercise. But I went up that one with the agility and grace of sixteen. Melissa followed me, and we found ourselves on the roof — fortunately it was a flat one — panting and gasping, but safe, unless that diabolical dog could climb a ladder.

I crept cautiously to the edge and peered over. The beast was sitting on his haunches at the foot of the ladder, and it was quite evident he was not short on time. The gleam in his eye seemed to say:

. "I've got you two unprincipled subscription hunters beautifully treed and it's treed you're going to stay. That is what I call satisfying."

I reported the state of the case to Melissa.

"What shall we do?" I asked.

"Do?" said Melissa, snappishly. "Why, stay here till Isaac Appleby comes out and takes that brute away? What else can we do?"

"What if he isn't at home?" I suggested.

"We'll stay here till he comes home. Oh, this is a nice predicament. This is what comes of cushioning churches!"

"It might be worse," I said comfortingly. "Suppose the roof hadn't been flat?"

"Call Isaac," said Melissa shortly.

I didn't fancy calling Isaac, but call him I did, and when that failed to bring him Melissa condescended to call, too; but scream as we might, no Isaac appeared, and that dog sat there and smiled internally.

"It's no use," said Melissa sulkily at last. "Isaac Appleby is dead or away."

Half an hour passed; it seemed as long as a day. The sun just boiled down on that roof and we were nearly melted. We were dreadfully thirsty, and the heat made our heads ache, and I could see my muslin dress fading before my very eyes. As for the roses on my best hat — but that was too harrowing to think about.

Then we saw a welcome sight — Isaac Appleby coming through the yard with a hoe over his shoulder. He had probably been working in his field at the back of the house. I never thought I should have been so glad to see him.

"Isaac, oh, Isaac!" I called joyfully, leaning over as far as I dared.

Isaac looked up in amazement at me and Melissa craning our necks over the edge of the roof. Then he saw the dog and took in the situation. The creature actually grinned.

"Won't you call off your dog and let us get down, Isaac?" I said pleadingly.

Isaac stood and reflected for a moment or two. Then he came slowly forward and, before we realized what he was going to do, he took that ladder down and laid it on the ground.

"Isaac Appleby, what do you mean?" demanded Melissa wrathfully.

Isaac folded his arms and looked up. It would be hard to say which face was the more determined, his or the dog's. But Isaac had the advantage in point of looks, I will say that for him.

"I mean that you two women will stay up on that roof until one of you agrees to marry me," said Isaac solemnly.

I gasped.

"Isaac Appleby, you can't be in earnest?" I cried incredulously. "You couldn't be so mean?"

"I am in earnest. I want a wife, and I am going to have one. You two will stay up there, and Julius Caesar here will watch you until one of you makes up her mind to take me. You can settle it between yourselves, and let me know when you have come to a decision."

And with that Isaac walked jauntily into his new house.

"The man can't mean it!" said Melissa. "He is trying to play a joke on us."

"He does mean it," I said gloomily. "An Appleby never says anything he doesn't mean. He will keep us here until one of us consents to marry him."

"It won't be me, then," said Melissa in a calm sort of rage. "I won't marry him if I have to sit on this roof for the rest of my life. You can take him. It's really you he wants, anyway; he asked you first."

I always knew that rankled with Melissa.

I thought the situation over before I said anything more. We certainly couldn't get off that roof, and if we could, there was Julius Caesar. The place was out of sight of every other house in Jersey Cove, and nobody might come near it for a week. To be sure, when Melissa and I didn't turn up the Covites might get out and search for us; but that wouldn't be for two or three days anyhow.

Melissa had turned her back on me and was sitting with her elbows propped up on her knees, looking gloomily out to sea. I was afraid I couldn't coax her into marrying Isaac. As for me, I hadn't any real objection to marrying him, after all, for if he was short of romance he was good-natured and had a fat bank account;* but I hated to be driven into it that way.

"You'd better take him, Melissa," I said entreatingly. "I've had one husband and that is enough."

---
*Change of tense from "is good-natured and has a fat bank account."

"More than enough for me, thank you," said Melissa sarcastically.

"Isaac is a fine man and has a lovely house; and you aren't sure the Kingsbridge man really means anything," I went on.

"I would rather," said Melissa, with the same awful calmness, "jump down from this roof and break my neck, or be devoured piecemeal by that fiend down there than marry Isaac Appleby."

It didn't seem worth while to say anything more after that. We sat there in stony silence and the time dragged by. I was hot, hungry, thirsty, cross; and besides, I felt that I was in a ridiculous position, which was worse than all the rest. We could see Isaac sitting in the shade of one of his apple trees in the front orchard comfortably reading a newspaper. I think if he hadn't aggravated me by doing that I'd have given in sooner. But as it was, I was determined to be as stubborn as everybody else. We were four obstinate creatures — Isaac and Melissa and Julius Caesar and I.

At four o'clock Isaac got up and went into the house; in a few minutes he came out again with a basket in one hand and a ball of cord in the other.

"I don't intend to starve you, of course, ladies," he said politely, "I will throw this ball up to you and you can then draw up the basket."

I caught the ball, for Melissa never turned her head. I would have preferred to be scornful, too, and reject the food altogether; but I was so dreadfully thirsty that I put my pride in my pocket and hauled the basket up. Besides, I thought it might enable us to hold out until some loophole of escape presented itself.

Isaac went back into the house and I unpacked the basket. There was a bottle of milk, some bread and butter, and a pie. Melissa wouldn't take a morsel of the food, but she was so thirsty she had to take a drink of milk.

She tried to lift her veil — and something caught;

Melissa gave it a savage twitch, and off came veil and hat — and all her front hair!

You never saw such a sight. I'd always suspected Melissa wore a false front, but I'd never had any proof before.

Melissa pinned on her hair again and put on her hat and drank the milk, all without a word; but she was purple. I felt sorry for her.

And I felt sorry for Isaac when I tried to eat that bread. It was sour and dreadful. As for the pie, it was hopeless. I tasted it, and then threw it down to Julius Caesar. Julius Caesar, not being over particular, ate it up. I thought perhaps it would kill him, for anything might come of eating such a concoction. That pie was a strong argument for Isaac. I thought a man who had to live on such cookery did indeed need a wife and might be pardoned for taking desperate measures to get one. I was dreadfully tired of broiling on the roof anyhow.

But it was the thunderstorm that decided me. When I saw it coming up, black and quick, from the northwest, I gave in at once. I had endured a good deal and was prepared to endure more; but I had paid ten dollars for my hat and I was not going to have it ruined by a thunderstorm. I called to Isaac and out he came.

"If you will let us down and promise to dispose of that dog before I come here I will marry you, Isaac," I said, "but I'll make you sorry for it afterwards, though."

"I'll take the risk of that, Anne," he said; "and, of course, I'll sell the dog. I won't need him when I have you."

Isaac meant to be complimentary, though you mightn't have thought so if you had seen the face of that dog.

Isaac ordered Julius Caesar away and put up the ladder, and turned his back, real considerately, while we climbed down. We had to go in his house and stay till the shower was over. I didn't forget the object of our call and I produced our subscription list at once.

"How much have you got?" asked Isaac.

"Seventy dollars and we want a hundred and fifty," I said.

"You may put me down for the remaining eighty, then," said Isaac calmly.

The Applebys are never mean where money is concerned, I must say.

Isaac offered to drive us home when it cleared up, but I said "No." I wanted to settle Melissa before she got a chance to talk.

On the way home I said to her:

"I hope you won't mention this to anyone, Melissa. I don't mind marrying Isaac, but I don't want people to know how it came about."

"Oh, I won't say anything about it," said Melissa, laughing a little disagreeably.

"Because," I said, to clinch the matter, looking significantly at her front hair as I said it, "I have something to tell, too."

Melissa will hold her tongue.

Akin
To Love

David Hartley had dropped in to pay a neighbourly call on Josephine Elliott. It was well along in the afternoon, and outside, in the clear crispness of a Canadian winter, the long blue shadows from the tall firs behind the house were falling over the snow.

It was a frosty day, and all the windows of every room where there was no fire were covered with silver palms. But the big, bright kitchen was warm and cosy, and somehow seemed to David more tempting than ever before, and that is saying a good deal. He had an uneasy feeling that he had stayed long enough and ought to go. Josephine was knitting at a long gray sock with doubly aggressive energy, and that was a sign that she was talked out. As long as Josephine had plenty to say, her plump white fingers, where her mother's wedding ring was lost in dimples, moved slowly among her needles. When conversation flagged she fell to her work as furiously as if a husband and half a dozen sons were waiting for its completion. David often wondered in his secret soul what Josephine did with all the interminable gray socks she knitted. Sometimes he concluded that she put them in the home missionary barrels; again, that she sold them to her hired man. At any rate, they were very warm and comfortable looking, and David sighed as he thought of the deplorable state his own socks were generally in.

When David sighed Josephine took alarm. She was afraid David was going to have one of his attacks of foolishness. She must head him off someway, so she rolled up the gray sock, stabbed the big pudgy ball with her needles, and said she guessed she'd get the tea.

David got up.

"Now, you're not going before tea?" said Josephine hospitably. "I'll have it all ready in no time."

"I ought to go home, I s'pose," said David, with the air and tone of a man dallying with a great temptation. "Zillah'll be waiting tea for me; and there's the stock to tend to."

"I guess Zillah won't wait long," said Josephine. She did not intend it at all, but there was a certain scornful ring in her voice. "You must stay. I've a fancy for company to tea."

David sat down again. He looked so pleased that Josephine went down on her knees behind the stove, ostensibly to get a stick of firewood, but really to hide her smile.

"I suppose he's tickled to death to think of getting a good square meal, after the starvation rations Zillah puts him on," she thought.

But Josephine misjudged David just as much as he misjudged her. She had really asked him to stay to tea out of pity, but David thought it was because she was lonesome, and he hailed that as an encouraging sign. And he was not thinking about getting a good meal either, although his dinner had been such a one as only Zillah Hartley could get up. As he leaned back in his cushioned chair and watched Josephine bustling about the kitchen, he was glorying in the fact that he could spend another hour with her, and sit opposite to her at the table while she poured his tea for him and passed him the biscuits, just as if — just as if —

Here Josephine looked straight at him with such intent and stern brown eyes that David felt she must have read his thoughts, and he colored guiltily. But Josephine did not even notice that he was blushing. She had only paused to wonder whether she would bring out cherry or strawberry preserve; and, having decided on the cherry, took her piercing gaze from David without having seen him at all. But he allowed his thoughts no more vagaries.

Josephine set the table with her mother's wedding china. She used it because it was the anniversary of her mother's wedding day, but David thought it was out of compliment to him. And, as he knew quite well that Josephine prized that china beyond all her other earthly possessions, he stroked his smooth-shaven, dimpled chin with the air of a man to whom is offered a very subtly sweet homage.

Josephine whisked in and out of the pantry, and up and down cellar, and with every whisk a new dainty was added to the table. Josephine, as everybody in Meadowby admitted, was past mistress in the noble art of cookery. Once upon a time rash matrons and ambitious young wives had aspired to rival her, but they had long ago realised the vanity of such efforts and dropped comfortably back to second place.

Josephine felt an artist's pride in her table when she set the teapot on its stand and invited David to sit in. There were pink slices of cold tongue, and crisp green pickles and spiced gooseberry, the recipe for which Josephine had invented herself, and which had taken first prize at the Provincial Exhibition for six successive years; there was a lemon pie which was a symphony in gold and silver, biscuits as light and white as snow, and moist, plummy cubes of fruit cake. There was the ruby-tinted cherry preserve, a mound of amber jelly, and, to crown all, steaming cups of tea, in flavour and fragrance unequalled.

And Josephine, too, sitting at the head of the table, with her smooth, glossy crimps of black hair and cheeks as rosy clear as they had been twenty years ago, when she had been a slender slip of girlhood and bashful young David Hartley had looked at her over his hymn-book in prayer-meeting and tramped all the way home a few feet behind her, because he was too shy to go boldly up and ask if he might see her home.

All taken together, what wonder if David lost his head

92

over that tea-table and determined to ask Josephine the same old question once more? It was eighteen years since he had asked it for the first time, and two years since the last. He would try his luck again; Josephine was certainly more gracious than he remembered her to ever have been before.

When the meal was over Josephine cleared the table and washed the dishes. When she had taken a dry towel and sat down by the window to polish her china David understood that his opportunity had come. He moved over and sat down beside her on the sofa by the window.

Outside the sun was setting in a magnificent arch of light and colour over the snow-clad hills and deep blue St. Lawrence gulf. David grasped at the sunset as an introductory factor.

"Isn't that fine, Josephine?" he said admiringly. "It makes me think of that piece of poetry that used to be in the old Fifth Reader when we went to school. D'ye mind how the teacher used to drill us up in it on Friday afternoons? It begun

'Slow sinks more lovely ere his race is run
Along Morea's hills the setting sun.'"

Then David declaimed the whole passage in a sing-song tone, accompanied by a few crude gestures recalled from long-ago school-boy elocution. Josephine knew what was coming. Every time David proposed to her he had begun by reciting poetry. She twirled her towel around the last plate resignedly. If it had to come, the sooner it was over the better. Josephine knew by experience that there was no heading David off, despite his shyness, when he had once got along as far as the poetry.

"But it's going to be for the last time," she said determinedly. "I'm going to settle this question so decidedly to-night that there'll never be a repetition."

When David had finished his quotation he laid his hand on Josephine's plump arm.

"Josephine," he said huskily, "I s'pose you couldn't —

could you now? — make up your mind to have me. I wish you would, Josephine — I wish you would. Don't you think you could, Josephine?"

Josephine folded up her towel, crossed her hands on it, and looked her wooer squarely in the eyes.

"David Hartley," she said deliberately, "what makes you go on asking me to marry you every once in a while when I've told you times out of mind that I can't and won't?"

"Because I can't help hoping that you'll change your mind through time," David replied meekly.

"Well, you just listen to me. I will not marry you. That is in the first place. And in the second, this is to be final. It has to be. You are never to ask me this again under any circumstances. If you do I will not answer you — I will not let on I hear you at all; but (and Josephine spoke very slowly and impressively) I will never speak to you again — never. We are good friends now, and I like you real well, and like to have you drop in for a neighbourly chat as often as you wish to, but there'll be an end, short and sudden, to that, if you don't mind what I say."

"Oh, Josephine, ain't that rather hard?" protested David feebly. It seemed terrible to be cut off from all hope with such finality as this.

"I mean every word of it," returned Josephine calmly. "You'd better go home now, David. I always feel as if I'd like to be alone for a spell after a disagreeable experience."

David obeyed sadly and put on his cap and overcoat. Josephine kindly warned him not to slip and break his legs on the porch, because the floor was as icy as anything; and she even lighted a candle and held it up at the kitchen door to guide him safely out. David, as he trudged sorrowfully homeward across the fields, carried with him the mental picture of a plump, sonsy woman, in a trim dress of plum-coloured homespun and ruffled blue-check apron, haloed by candlelight. It was not a very romantic vision, perhaps, but to David it was more beautiful than anything else in the world.

When David was gone Josephine shut the door with a little shiver. She blew out the candle, for it was not yet dark enough to justify artificial light to her thrifty mind. She thought the big, empty house, in which she was the only living thing, was very lonely. It was so still, except for the slow tick of the "grandfather's clock" and the soft purr and crackle of the wood in the stove. Josephine sat down by the window.

"I wish some of the Sentners would run down," she said aloud. "If David hadn't been so ridiculous I'd have got him to stay the evening. He can be good company when he likes — he's real well-read and intelligent. And he must have dismal times at home there with nobody but Zillah."

She looked across the yard to the little house at the other side of it, where her French-Canadian hired man lived, and watched the purple spiral of smoke from its chimney curling up against the crocus sky. Would she run over and see Mrs. Leon Poirier and her little black-eyed, brown-skinned baby? No, they never knew what to say to each other.

"If 'twasn't so cold I'd go up and see Ida," she said. "As it is, I guess I'd better fall back on my knitting, for I saw Jimmy Sentner's toes sticking through his socks the other day. How setback poor David did look, to be sure! But I think I've settled that marrying notion of his once for all and I'm glad of it."

She said the same thing next day to Mrs. Tom Sentner, who had come down to help her pick her geese. They were at work in the kitchen with a big tubful of feathers between them, and on the table a row of dead birds, which Leon had killed and brought in. Josephine was enveloped in a shapeless print wrapper, and had an apron tied tightly around her head to keep the down out of her beautiful hair, of which she was rather proud.

"What do you think, Ida?" she said, with a hearty laugh at the recollection. "David Hartley was here to tea last night, and asked me to marry him again. There's a persistent man for you. I can't brag of ever having had many beaux, but I've certainly had my fair share of proposals."

Mrs. Tom did not laugh. Her thin little face, with its faded prettiness, looked as if she never laughed.

"Why won't you marry him?" she said fretfully.

"Why should I?" retorted Josephine. "Tell me that, Ida Sentner."

"Because it is high time you were married," said Mrs. Tom decisively. "I don't believe in women living single. And I don't see what better you can do than take David Hartley."

Josephine looked at her sister with the interested expression of a person who is trying to understand some mental attitude in another which is a standing puzzle to her. Ida's evident wish to see her married always amused Josephine. Ida had married very young and for fifteen years her life had been one of drudgery and ill-health. Tom Sentner was a lazy, shiftless fellow. He neglected his family and was drunk half his time. Meadowby people said that he beat his wife when "on the spree," but Josephine did not believe that, because she did not think that Ida could keep from telling her if it were so. Ida Sentner was not given to bearing her trials in silence.

Had it not been for Josephine's assistance, Tom Sentner's family would have stood an excellent chance of starvation. Josephine practically kept them, and her generosity never failed or stinted. She fed and clothed her nephews and nieces, and all the gray socks whose destination puzzled David so much went to the Sentners.

As for Josephine herself, she had a good farm, a comfortable house, a plump bank account, and was an independent, unworried woman. And yet, in the face of all this, Mrs. Tom Sentner could bewail the fact that Josephine had no husband to look out for her. Josephine shrugged her shoulders and gave up the conundrum, merely saying ironically, in reply to her sister's remark:

"And go to live with Zillah Hartley?"

"You know very well you wouldn't have to do that. Ever since John Hartley's wife at the Creek died he's been wanting Zillah to go and keep house for him, and if David got married Zillah'd go quick. Catch her staying there if you were mistress! And David has such a beautiful house! It's ten times finer than yours, though I don't deny yours is comfortable. And his farm is the best in Meadowby and joins yours. Think what a beautiful property they'd make together. You're all right now, Josephine, but what will you do when you get old and have nobody to take care of you? I declare the thought worries me at night till I can't sleep."

"I should have thought you had enough worries of your own to keep you awake at nights without taking over any of mine," said Josephine drily. "As for old age, it's a good ways off for me yet. When your Jack gets old enough to have some sense he can come here and live with me. But I'm not going to marry David Hartley, you can depend on that, Ida, my dear. I wish you could have heard him rhyming off that poetry last night. It doesn't seem to matter much what piece he recites — first thing that comes into his head, I reckon. I remember one time he went clean through that hymn beginning, 'Hark from the tombs a doleful sound,' and two years ago it was 'To Mary in Heaven,' as lackadaisical as you please. I never had such a time to keep from laughing, but I managed it, for I wouldn't hurt his feelings for the world. No, I haven't any intention of marrying anybody, but if I had it wouldn't be dear old sentimental, easy-going David."

Mrs. Tom thumped a plucked goose down on the bench with an expression which said that she, for one, wasn't going to waste any more words on an idiot. Easy-going, indeed! Did Josephine consider that a drawback? Mrs. Tom sighed. If Josephine, she thought, had put up with Tom Sentner's tempers for fifteen years she would know how to appreciate a good-natured man at his real value.

The cold snap which had set in on the day of David's

call lasted and deepened for a week. On Saturday evening, when Mrs. Tom came down for a jug of cream, the mercury of the little thermometer thumping against Josephine's porch was below zero. The gulf was no longer blue, but white with ice. Everything outdoors was crackling and snapping. Inside Josephine had kept roaring fires all through the house but the only place really warm was the kitchen.

"Wrap your head up well, Ida," she said anxiously, when Mrs. Tom rose to go. "You've got a bad cold."

"There's a cold going," said Mrs. Tom. "Everyone has it. David Hartley was up at our place to-day barking terrible — a real churchyard cough, as I told him. He never takes any care of himself. He said Zillah had a bad cold, too. Won't she be cranky while it lasts?"

Josephine sat up late that night to keep fires on. She finally went to bed in the little room opposite the big hall stove, and she slept at once, and dreamed that the thumps of the thermometer flapping in the wind against the wall outside grew louder and more insistent until they woke her up. Some one was pounding on the porch door.

Josephine sprang out of bed and hurried on her wrapper and felt shoes. She had no doubt that some of the Sentners were sick. They had a habit of getting sick about that time of night. She hurried out and opened the door, expecting to see hulking Tom Sentner, or perhaps Ida herself, big eyed and hysterical.

But David Hartley stood there, panting for breath. The clear moonlight showed that he had no overcoat on, and he was coughing hard. Josephine, before she spoke a word, clutched him by the arm and pulled him in out of the wind.

"For pity's sake, David Hartley, what is the matter?"

"Zillah's awful sick," he gasped. "I came here because 'twas nearest. Oh, won't you come over, Josephine? I've got to go for the doctor and I can't leave her alone. She's suffering dreadful. I know you and her ain't on good terms, but you'll come, won't you?"

"Of course I will," said Josephine sharply. "I'm not a barbarian, I hope, to refuse to go to the help of a sick person, if 'twas my worst enemy. I'll go in and get ready and you go straight to the hall stove and warm yourself. There's a good fire in it yet. What on earth do you mean, starting out on a bitter night like this without an overcoat or even mittens, and you with a cold like that?"

"I never thought of them, I was so frightened," said David apologetically. "I just lit up a fire in the kitchen stove as quick's I could and run. It rattled me to hear Zillah moaning so's you could hear her all over the house."

"You need someone to look after you as bad as Zillah does," said Josephine severely.

In a very few minutes she was ready, with a basket packed full of homely remedies, "for like as not there'll be no putting one's hand on anything there," she muttered. She insisted on wrapping her big plaid shawl around David's head and neck, and made him put on a pair of mittens she had knitted for Jack Sentner. Then she locked the door and they started across the gleaming, crusted field. It was so slippery that Josephine had to cling to David's arm to keep her feet. In the rapture of supporting her David almost forgot everything else.

In a few minutes they had passed under the bare, glistening boughs of the poplars on David's lawn, and for the first time Josephine crossed the threshold of David Hartley's house.

Years ago, in her girlhood, when the Hartley's lived in the old house and there were half a dozen girls at home, Josephine had frequently visited there. All the Hartley girls liked her except Zillah. She and Zillah never "got on" together. When the other girls had married and gone, Josephine gave up visiting there. She had never been inside the new house, and she and Zillah had not spoken to each other for years.

Zillah was a sick woman — too sick to be anything but civil to Josephine. David started at once for the doctor at the Creek, and Josephine saw that he was well wrapped up before she let him go. Then she mixed up a mustard plaster for Zillah and sat down by the bedside to wait.

When Mrs. Tom Sentner came down the next day she found Josephine busy making flaxseed poultices, with her lips set in a line that betokened she had made up her mind to some disagreeable course of duty.

"Zillah has got pneumonia bad," she said, in reply to Mrs. Tom's inquiries. "The Doctor is here and Mary Bell from the Creek. She'll wait on Zillah, but there'll have to be another woman here to see to the work. I reckon I'll stay. I suppose it's my duty and I don't see who else could be got. You can send Mamie and Jack down to stay at my house until I can go back. I'll run over every day and keep an eye on things."

At the end of a week Zillah was out of danger. Saturday afternoon Josephine went over home to see how Mamie and Jack were getting on. She found Mrs. Tom there, and the latter promptly despatched Jack and Mamie to the post-office that she might have an opportunity to hear Josephine's news.

"I've had an awful week of it, Ida," said Josephine solemnly, as she sat down by the stove and put her feet up on the glowing hearth.

"I suppose Zillah is pretty cranky to wait on," said Mrs. Tom sympathetically.

"Oh, it isn't Zillah. Mary Bell looks after her. No, it's the house. I never lived in such a place of dust and disorder in my born days. I'm sorrier for David Hartley than I ever was for anyone before."

"I suppose he's used to it," said Mrs. Tom with a shrug.

"I don't see how anyone could ever get used to it," groaned Josephine. "And David used to be so particular when he was a boy. The minute I went there the other night I took in that kitchen with a look. I don't believe the

100

paint has even been washed since the house was built. I honestly don't. And I wouldn't like to be called upon to swear when the floor was scrubbed either. The corners were just full of rolls of dust — you could have shovelled it out. I swept it out next day and I thought I'd be choked. As for the pantry — well, the less said about *that* the better. And it's the same all through the house. You could write your name on everything. I couldn't so much as clean up. Zillah was so sick there couldn't be a bit of noise made. I did manage to sweep and dust, and I cleaned out the pantry. And, of course, I saw that the meals were nice and well cooked. You should have seen David's face. He looked as if he couldn't get used to having things clean and tasty. I darned his socks — he hadn't a whole pair to his name — and I've done everything I could to give him a little comfort. Not that I could do much. If Zillah heard me moving round she'd send Mary Bell out to ask what the matter was. When I wanted to go upstairs I'd have to take off my shoes and tiptoe up on my stocking feet, so's she wouldn't know it. And I'll have to stay there another fortnight yet. Zillah won't be able to sit up till then. I don't really know if I can stand it without falling to and scrubbing the house from garret to cellar in spite of her."

Mrs. Tom Sentner did not say much to Josephine. To herself she said complacently:

"She's sorry for David. Well, I've always heard that pity was akin to love. We'll see what comes of this."

Josephine did manage to live through that fortnight. One morning she remarked to David at the breakfast table:

"Well, I think that Mary Bell will be able to attend to the work after today, David. I guess I'll go home tonight."

David's face clouded over.

"Well, I s'pose we oughtn't to keep you any longer, Josephine. I'm sure it's been awful good of you to stay this long. I don't know what we'd have done without you."

"You're welcome," said Josephine shortly.

"Don't go for to walk home," said David; "the snow is too deep. I'll drive you over when you want to go."

"I'll not go before the evening," said Josephine slowly.

David went out to his work gloomily. For three weeks he had been living in comfort. His wants were carefully attended to; his meals were well cooked and served, and everything was bright and clean. And more than all, Josephine had been there, with her cheerful smile and companionable ways. Well, it was all ended now.

Josephine sat at the breakfast table long after David had gone out. She scowled at the sugar-bowl and shook her head savagely at the tea-pot.

"I'll have to do it," she said at last.

"I'm so sorry for him that I can't do anything else."

She got up and went to the window, looking across the snowy field to her own home, nestled between the grove of firs and the orchard.

"It's awful snug and comfortable," she said regretfully, "and I've always felt set on being free and independent. But it's no use. I'd never have a minute's peace of mind again, thinking of David living here in dirt and disorder, and him so particular and tidy by nature. No, it's my duty, plain and clear, to come here and make things pleasant for him — the pointing of Providence, as you might say. The worst of it is, I'll have to tell him so myself. He'll never dare to mention the subject again, after what I said to him that night he proposed last. I wish I hadn't been so dreadful emphatic. Now I've got to say it myself if it is ever said. But I'll not begin by quoting poetry, that's one thing sure!"

Josephine threw back her head, crowned with its shining braids of jet-black hair, and laughed heartily. She bustled back to the stove and poked up the fire.

"I'll have a bit of corned beef and cabbage for dinner," she said, "and I'll make David that pudding he's so fond of. After all, it's kind of nice to have someone to plan and think for. It always did seem like a waste of energy to fuss

102

over cooking things when there was nobody but myself to eat them.

Josephine sang over her work all day, and David went about his with the face of a man who is going to the gallows without benefit of clergy. When he came in to supper at sunset his expression was so woe-begone that Josephine had to dodge into the pantry to keep from laughing outright. She relieved her feelings by pounding the dresser with the potato masher, and then went primly out and took her place at the table.

The meal was not a success from a social point of view. Josephine was nervous and David glum. Mary Bell gobbled down her food with her usual haste, and then went away to carry Zillah hers. Then David said reluctantly:

"If you want to go home now, Josephine, I'll hitch up Red Rob and drive you over."

Josephine began to plait the tablecloth. She wished again that she had not been so emphatic on the occasion of his last proposal. Without replying to David's suggestion she said crossly (Josephine always spoke crossly when she was especially in earnest) :

"I want to tell you what I think about Zillah. She's getting better, but she's had a terrible shaking up, and it's my opinion that she won't be good for much all winter. She won't be able to do any hard work, that's certain. If you want my advice, I tell you fair and square that I think she'd better go off for a visit as soon as she's fit. She thinks so herself. Clementine wants her to go and stay a spell with her in town. 'Twould be just the thing for her."

"She can go if she wants to, of course," said David dully. "I can get along by myself for a spell."

"There's no need of your getting along by yourself," said Josephine, more crossly than ever. "I'll — I'll come here and keep house for you if you like."

David looked at her uncomprehendingly.

"Wouldn't people kind of gossip?" he asked hesitatingly. "Not but what—"

"I don't see what they'd have to gossip about," broke in Josephine, "if we were—married."

David sprang to his feet with such haste that he almost upset the table.

"Josephine, do you mean that?" he exclaimed.

"Of course I mean it," she said, in a perfectly savage tone. "Now, for pity's sake, don't say another word about it just now. I can't discuss it for a spell. Go out to your work. I want to be alone for awhile."

For the first and last time David disobeyed her. Instead of going out, he strode around the table, caught Josephine masterfully in his arms, and kissed her. And Josephine, after a second's hesitation, kissed him in return.

# The
Finished Story

She always sat in a corner of the west veranda
at the hotel, knitting something white and fluffy, or pink
and fluffy, or pale blue and fluffy — always fluffy, at least,
and always dainty. Shawls and scarfs and hoods the things
were, I believe. When she finished one she gave it to some
girl and began another. Every girl at Harbour Light that
summer wore some distracting thing that had been fashioned by Miss Sylvia's slim, tireless, white fingers.

She was old, with that beautiful, serene old age which
is as beautiful in its way as youth. Her girlhood and
womanhood must have been very lovely to have ripened
into such a beauty of sixty years. It was a surprise to everyone who heard her called *Miss* Sylvia. She looked so like a
woman who ought to have stalwart, grown sons and
dimpled little grandchildren.

For the first two days after the arrival at the hotel she
sat in her corner alone. There was always a circle of young
people around her; old folks and middle-aged people
would have liked to join it, but Miss Sylvia, while she was
gracious to all, let it be distinctly understood that her
sympathies were with youth. She sat among the boys and
girls, young men and maidens, like a fine white queen. Her
dress was always the same and somewhat old-fashioned,
but nothing else would have suited her half so well; she
wore a lace cap on her snowy hair and a heliotrope shawl
over her black silk shoulders. She knitted continually and
talked a good deal, but listened more. We sat around her
at all hours of the day and told her everything.

When you were first introduced to her you called her

105

Miss Stanleymain. Her endurance of that was limited to twenty-four hours. Then she begged you to call her Miss Sylvia, and as Miss Sylvia you spoke and thought of her forevermore.

Miss Sylvia liked us all, but I was her favourite. She told us so frankly and let it be understood that when I was talking to her and her heliotrope shawl was allowed to slip under one arm it was a sign that we were not to be interrupted. I was as vain of her favour as any lovelorn suitor whose lady had honoured him, not knowing, as I came to know later, the reason for it.

Although Miss Sylvia had an unlimited capacity for receiving confidences, she never gave any. We were all sure that there must be some romance in her life, but our efforts to discover it were unsuccessful. Miss Sylvia parried tentative questions so skilfully that we knew she had something to defend. But one evening, when I had known her a month, as time is reckoned, and long years as affection and understanding are computed, she told me her story — at least, what there was to tell of it. The last chapter was missing.

We were sitting together on the veranda at sunset. Most of the hotel people had gone for a harbour sail; a few forlorn mortals prowled about the grounds and eyed our corner wistfully, but by the sign of the heliotrope shawl knew it was not for them.

I was reading one of my stories to Miss Sylvia. In my own excuse I must allege that she tempted me to do it. I did not go around with manuscripts under my arm, inflicting them on defenceless females. But Miss Sylvia had discovered that I was a magazine scribbler, and moreover, that I had shut myself up in my room that very morning and perpetrated a short story. Nothing would do but that I read it to her.

It was a rather sad little story. The hero loved the heroine, and she loved him. There was no reason why he should not love her, but there was a reason why he could not marry her. When he found that he loved her he knew that he must go away. But might he not, at least, tell her his love? Might he not, at least, find out for his consolation if she cared for him? There was a struggle; he won, and went away without a word, believing it to be the more manly course. When I began to read Miss Sylvia was knitting, a pale green something this time, of the tender hue of young leaves in May. But after a little her knitting slipped unheeded to her lap and her hands folded idly above it. It was the most subtle compliment I had ever received.

When I turned the last page of the manuscript and looked up, Miss Sylvia's soft brown eyes were full of tears. She lifted her hands, clasped them together and said in an agitated voice:

"Oh, no, no; don't let him go away without telling her — just telling her. Don't let him do it!"

"But, you see, Miss Sylvia," I explained, flattered beyond measure that my characters had seemed so real to her, "that would spoil the story. It would have no reason for existence then. Its *motif* is simply his mastery over self. He believes it to be the nobler course."

"No, no, it wasn't — if he loved her he should have told her. Think of her shame and humiliation — she loved him, and he went without a word and she could never know he cared for her. Oh, you must change it — you must, indeed! I cannot bear to think of her suffering what I have suffered."

Miss Sylvia broke down and sobbed. To appease her, I promised that I would remodel the story, although I knew that the doing so would leave it absolutely pointless.

"Oh, I'm so glad," said Miss Sylvia, her eyes shining through her tears. "You see, I know it would make her happier — I know it. I'm going to tell you my poor little story to convince you. But you — you must not tell it to any of the others."

"I am sorry you think the admonition necessary," I said reproachfully.

"Oh, I do not, indeed I do not," she hastened to assure me. "I know I can trust you. But it's such a poor little story. You mustn't laugh at it — it is all the romance I had. Years ago — forty years ago — when I was a young girl of twenty, I—learned to care very much for somebody. I met him at a summer resort like this. I was there with my aunt and he was there with his mother, who was delicate. We saw a great deal of each other for a little while. He was —oh, he was like no other man I had ever seen. You remind me of him somehow. That is partly why I like you so much. I noticed the resemblance the first time I saw you. I don't know in just what it consists — in your expression and the way you carry your head, I think. He was not strong — he coughed a good deal. Then one day he went away — suddenly. I had thought he cared for me, but he never said so — just went away. Oh, the shame of it! After a time I heard that he had been ordered to California for his health. And he died out there the next spring. My heart broke then, I never cared for anybody again — I couldn't. I have always loved him. But it would have been so much easier to bear if I had only known that he loved me — oh, it would have made all the difference in the world. And the sting of it has been there all these years. I can't even permit myself the joy of dwelling on his memory because of the thought that perhaps he did not care."

"He must have cared," I said warmly. "He couldn't have helped it, Miss Sylvia."

Miss Sylvia shook her head with a sad smile.

"I cannot be sure. Sometimes I think he did. But then the doubt creeps back again. I would give almost anything to know that he did — to know that I have not lavished all the love of my life on a man who did not want it. And I never can know, never — I can hope and almost believe, but I can never know. Oh, you don't understand — a man couldn't fully understand what my pain has been over it. You see now why I want you to change the story. I am sorry for that poor girl, but if you only let her know that he really loves her she will not mind all the rest so very much; she will be able to bear the pain of even life-long separation if she only knows."

Miss Sylvia picked up her knitting and went away. As for me, I thought savagely of the dead man she loved and called him a cad, or at best, a fool.

Next day Miss Sylvia was her serene, smiling self once more, and she did not again make any reference to what she had told me. A fortnight later she returned home and I went my way back to the world. During the following winter I wrote several letters to Miss Sylvia and received replies from her. Her letters were very like herself. When I sent her the third-rate magazine containing my story — nothing but a third-rate magazine would take it in its rewritten form — she wrote to say that she was so glad that I had let the poor girl know.

Early in April I received a letter from an aunt of mine in the country, saying that she intended to sell her place and come to the city to live. She asked me to go out to Sweetwater for a few weeks and assist her in the business of settling up the estate and disposing of such things as she did not wish to take with her.

When I arrived at Sweetwater I found it moist and chill with the sunny moisture and teasing chill of our Canadian springs. They are long and fickle and reluctant, these springs of ours, but, oh, the unnamable charm of them! There was something even in the red buds of the maples at Sweetwater and in the long, smoking stretches of hillside fields that sent a thrill through my veins, finer and subtler than any given by old wine.

A week after my arrival, when we had got the larger affairs pretty well straightened out, Aunt Mary suggested that I had better overhaul Uncle Alan's room.

"The things there have never been meddled with since he died," she said. "In particular, there's an old trunk full of his letters and his papers. It was brought home from California after his death. I've never examined them. I don't suppose there is anything of any importance among them. But I'm not going to carry all that old rubbish to town. So I wish you would look over them and see if there is anything that should be kept. The rest may be burned."

I felt no particular interest in the task. My Uncle Alan Blair was a mere name to me. He was my mother's eldest brother and had died years before I was born. I had heard that he had been very clever and that great things had been expected of him. But I anticipated no pleasure from exploring musty old letters and papers of forty neglected years.

I went up to Uncle Alan's room at dusk that night. We had been having a day of warm spring rain, but it had cleared away and the bare maple boughs outside the window were strung with glistening drops. The room looked to the north and was always dim by reason of the close-growing Sweetwater pines. A gap had been cut through them to the northwest, and in it I had a glimpse of the sea Uncle Alan had loved, and above it a wondrous sunset sky fleeced over with little clouds, pale and pink and golden and green, that suddenly reminded me of Miss Sylvia and her fluffy knitting. It was with the thought of her in my mind that I lighted a lamp and began the task of grubbing into Uncle Alan's trunkful of papers. Most of these were bundles of yellowed letters, of no present interest, from his family and college friends. There were several college theses and essays, and a lot of loose miscellania pertaining to boyish school days. I went through the collection rapidly, until at the bottom of the trunk, I came to a small book bound in dark-green leather. It proved to be a sort of journal, and I began to glance over it with a languid interest.

It had been begun in the spring after he had graduated from college. Although suspected only by himself, the disease which was to end his life had already fastened upon him. The entries were those of a doomed man, who, feeling the curse fall on him like a frost, blighting all the fair hopes and promises of life, seeks some help and consolation in the outward self-communing of a journal. There was nothing morbid, nothing unmanly in the record. As I read, I found myself liking Uncle Alan, wishing that he might have lived and been my friend.

His mother had not been well that summer and the doctor ordered her to the seashore. Alan accompanied her. Here occurred a hiatus in the journal. No leaves had been torn out, but a quire or so of them had apparently become loosened from the threads that held them in place. I found them later on in the trunk, but at the time I passed to the next page. It began abruptly:

> This girl is the sweetest thing that God ever made. I had not known a woman could be so fair and sweet. Her beauty awes me, the purity of her soul shines so clearly through it like an illuminating lamp. I love her with all my power of loving and I am thankful that it is so. It would have been hard to die without having known love. I am glad that it has come to me, even if its price is unspeakable bitterness. A man has not lived for nothing who has known and loved Sylvia Stanleymain.
>
> I must not seek her love — that is denied me. If I were well and strong I should win it; yes, I believe I could win it, and nothing in the world would prevent me from trying, but, as things are, it would be the part of a coward to try. Yet I cannot resist the delight of being with her, of talking to her, of watching her wonderful face. She is in my thoughts day and night, she dwells in my dreams. O, Sylvia, I love you, my sweet!

A week later there was another entry:

> July Seventeenth.
>
> I am afraid. To-day I met Sylvia's eyes. In them was a look which at first stirred my heart to its deeps with tumultuous delight, and then I remembered. I must spare her that suffering, at whatever cost to myself. I must not let myself dwell on the dangerous sweetness of the thought that her heart is turning to me. What would be the crowning joy to another man could be only added sorrow to me.

Then:

> July Eighteenth.
>
> This morning I took the train to the city. I was determined to know the worst once for all. The time had come when I must. My doctor at home had put me off with vague hopes and

perhapses. So I went to a noted physician in the city. I told him I wanted the whole truth — I made him tell it. Stripped of all softening verbiage it is this: I have perhaps eight months or a year to live — no more!

I had expected it, although not quite so soon. Yet the certainty was none the less bitter. But this is no time for self-pity. It is of Sylvia I must think now. I shall go away at once, before the sweet fancy which is possibly budding in her virgin heart shall have bloomed into a flower that might poison some of her fair years.

July Nineteenth.

It is over. I said good-bye to her to-day before others, for I dared not trust myself to see her alone. She looked hurt and startled, as if someone had struck her. But she will soon forget, even if I have not been mistaken in the reading of her eyes. As for me, the bitterness of death is already over in that parting. All that now remains is to play the man to the end.

From further entries in the journal I learned that Alan Blair had returned to Sweetwater and later on had been ordered to California. The entries during his sojourn there were few and far between. In all of them he spoke of Sylvia. Finally, after a long silence, he had written:

I think the end is not far off now. I am not sorry for my suffering has been great of late. Last night I was easier. I slept and dreamed that I saw Sylvia. Once or twice I thought that I would arrange to have this book sent to her after my death. But I have decided that it would be unwise. It would only pain her, so I shall destroy it when I feel the time has come.

It is sunset in this wonderful summer land. At home in Sweetwater it is only early spring as yet, with snow lingering along the edges of the woods. The sunsets there will be creamy-yellow and pale red now. If I could but see them once more! And Sylvia—

There was a little blot where the pen had fallen. Evidently the end had been nearer than Alan Blair had thought. At least, there were no more entries, and the little green book had not been destroyed. I was glad that it had not been; and I felt glad that it was thus put in my power to write the last chapter of Miss Sylvia's story for her.

As soon as I could leave Sweetwater I went to the city, three hundred miles away, where Miss Sylvia lived. I found her in her library, in her black silk dress and heliotrope shawl, knitting up cream wool, for all the world as if she had just been transplanted from the veranda corner of Harbour Light.

"My dear boy!" she said.

"Do you know why I have come?" I asked.

"I am vain enough to think it was because you wanted to see me," she smiled.

"I did want to see you; but I would have waited until summer if it had not been that I wished to bring you the missing chapter of your story, dear lady."

"I—I—don't understand," said Miss Sylvia, starting slightly.

"I had an uncle, Alan Blair, who died forty years ago in California," I said quietly. "Recently I have had occasion to examine some of his papers. I found a journal among them and I have brought it to you because I think that you have the best right to it."

I dropped the parcel in her lap. She was silent with surprise and bewilderment.

"And now," I added, "I am going away. You won't want to see me or anyone for a while after you have read this book. But I will come up to see you to-morrow."

When I went the next day Miss Sylvia herself met me at the door. She caught my hand and drew me into the hall. Her eyes were softly radiant.

"Oh, you have made me so happy!" she said tremulously. "Oh, you can never know how happy! Nothing hurts now — nothing ever can hurt, because I know he did care."

She laid her face down on my shoulder, as a girl might have nestled to her lover, and I bent and kissed her for Uncle Alan.

My
Lady Jane

The boat got into Broughton half an hour after the train had gone. We had been delayed by some small accident to the machinery; hence that lost half-hour, which meant a night's sojourn for me in Broughton. I am ashamed of the things I thought and said. When I think that fate might have taken me at my word and raised up a special train, or some such miracle, by which I might have got away from Broughton that night, I experience a cold chill. Out of gratitude I have never sworn over missing connections since.

At the time, however, I felt thoroughly exasperated. I was in a hurry to get on. Important business engagements would be unhinged by the delay. I was a stranger in Broughton. It looked like a stupid, stuffy little town. I went to a hotel in an atrocious humor. After I had fumed until I wanted a change, it occurred to me that I might as well hunt up Clark Oliver by way of passing the time. I had never been overly fond of Clark Oliver, although he was my cousin. He was a bit of a cad, and stupider than anyone belonging to our family had a right to be. Moreover, he was in politics, and I detest politics. But I rather wanted to see if he looked as much like me as he used to. I hadn't seen him for three years and I hoped that the time might have differentiated us to a saving degree. It was over a year since I had last been blown up by some unknown, excited individual on the ground that I was that scoundrel Oliver — politically speaking. I thought that was a good omen.

I went to Clark's office, found he had left, and followed

him to his rooms. The minute I saw him I experienced the same nasty feeling of lost or bewildered individuality which always overcame me in his presence. He was so absurdly like me. I felt as if I were looking into a mirror where my reflection persisted in doing things I didn't do, thereby producing a most uncanny sensation.

Clark pretended he was glad to see me. He really couldn't have been, because his Great Idea hadn't struck him then, and we had always disliked each other.

"Hello, Elliott," he said, shaking me by the hand with a twist he had learned in election campaigns, whereby something like heartiness was simulated. "Glad to see you, old fellow. Gad, you're as like me as ever. Where did you drop from?"

I explained my predicament and we talked amiably and harmlessly for awhile about family gossip. I abhor family gossip, but it is a shade better than politics, and those two subjects are the only ones on which Clark can converse at all. I described Mary Alice's wedding, and Florence's new young man, and Tom-and-Kate's twins. Clark tried to be interested but I saw he had something on what serves him for a mind. After awhile it came out. He looked at his watch with a frown.

"I'm in a bit of a puzzle," he said. "The Mark Kennedys are giving a dinner to-night. You don't know them, of course. They're the big people of Broughton. Kennedy runs the politics of the place, and Mrs. K. makes or mars people socially. It's my first invitation there and it's necessary I should accept it — necessary every way. Mrs. K. would never forgive me if I disappointed her at the last moment. Not that I, personally, am of much account — yet — to her. But it would leave a vacant place. Mrs. K. would never notice me again and, as she bosses Kennedy, I can't afford to offend her. Besides, there's a girl who'll be there. I've met her once. I want to meet her again. She's a beauty and no mistake. Toplofty as they make 'em, though. However, I think I've made an impression on her. It was at the Harvey's dance last week. She was the handsomest woman there, and she never took her eyes off me. I've given Mrs. Kennedy a pretty broad hint that I want to take her in to dinner. If I don't go I'll miss all round."

"Well, what is there to prevent you from going?" I asked, squiffily. I never could endure the way Clark talked about girls and hinted at his conquests.

"Just this. Herbert Bronson came to town this afternoon and is leaving on the 10.30 train to-night. He's sent me word to meet him at his hotel this evening and talk over a mining deal I've been trying to pull off. I simply must go. It's my one chance to corral Bronson. If I lose him it'll be all up, and I'll be thousands out of pocket."

"Well, you *are* in rather a predicament," I agreed, with the philosophical acceptance of the situation that marks the outsider. *I* wasn't hampered by the multiplicity of my business and social engagements that evening, so I could afford to pity Clark. It is always rather nice to be able to pity a person you dislike.

"I should say so. I can't make up my mind what to do. Hang it. I'll *have* to see Bronson. There's no question about that. A man ought to keep an understood substitute on hand to send to dinners when he can't go. By Jove! Elliott!"

Clark's Great Idea had arrived. He bounced up eagerly.

"Elliott, will *you* go to the Kennedys' in my place? They'll never know the difference. Do, now — there's a good fellow!"

"Nonsense!" I said.

"It isn't nonsense. The resemblance between us was fore-ordained for this hour. I'll lend you my dress suit — it'll fit you — your figure is as much like mine as your face. You've nothing to do with yourself this evening. I offer you a good dinner and an agreeable partner. Come now, to oblige me. You know you owe me a good turn for that Mulhenen business."

The Mulhenen business clinched the matter. Until he

mentioned it I had no notion whatever of masquerading as Clark Oliver at the Kennedys' dinner. But, as Clark so delicately put it, he had done me a good turn in that affair and the obligation had rankled ever since. It is beastly to be indebted for a favor to a man you detest. Now was my chance to pay it off and I took it without more ado.

"But," I said doubtfully, "I don't know the Kennedys — nor any of the social stunts that are doing in Broughton. I won't dare to talk about anything, and I'll seem so stupid, even if I don't actually make some irremediable blunder, that the Kennedys will be disgusted with you. It will probably do your prospects more harm than your absence would."

"Not at all. Keep your mouth shut when you can and talk generalities when you can't, and you'll pass. If you take that girl in she's a stranger in Broughton and won't suspect your ignorance of what's going on. Nobody will suspect you. Nobody here knows I have a cousin so like me. Our own mothers haven't always been able to tell us apart. Our very voices are alike. Come now, get into my dinner togs. You haven't much time and Mrs. K. doesn't like late comers."

There seemed to be a number of things that Mrs. Kennedy did not like. I thought my chance of pleasing that critical lady extremely small, especially when I had to live up to Clark Oliver's personality. However, I dressed as expeditiously as possible. The novelty of the adventure rather pleased me. I always liked doing unusual things. Anything was better than lounging away the evening at my hotel. It couldn't do any harm. I owed Clark Oliver a good turn and I would save Mrs. Kennedy the annoyance of a vacant chair.

There was no disputing the fact that I looked most disgustingly like Clark when I got into his clothes. I actually felt a grudge against them for their excellent fit.

"You'll do," said Clark. "Remember you're a Conservative to-night and don't let your rank Liberal views crop

117

out, or you'll queer me for all time with the great and only Mark. He doesn't talk politics at his dinners, though, so you're not likely to have trouble on that score. Mrs. Kennedy has a weakness for beer mugs. Her collection is considered very fine. Scandal whispers that Miss Harvey has a budding interest in settlement work—"

"Miss who?" I said sharply.

"Harvey. Christian name unknown. That's the girl I mentioned. You'll probably take her in. Be nice to her even if you have to make an effort. She's the one I've picked out as your future cousin, you know, so I don't want you to spoil her good opinion of me in any way."

The name had given me a jump. Once, in another world, I had known a Jane Harvey. But Clark's Miss Harvey couldn't be Jane. A month before I had read a newspaper item to the effect that Jane was on the Pacific coast. Moreover, Jane, when I knew her, had certainly no manifest vocation for settlement work. I didn't think two years could have worked such a transformation. Two years! Was it only two years? It seemed more like two centuries.

I went to the Kennedys' in a pleasantly excited frame of mind and a cab. I just missed being late by a hairbreadth. The house was a big one, and everybody pertaining to it was big, except the host. Mark Kennedy was a little, thin man with a bald head. He didn't look like a political power, but that was all the more reason for his being one in a world where things are not what they seem.

Mrs. Kennedy greeted me cordially and told me significantly that she had granted my request. This meant, as my card had already informed me, that I was to take Miss Harvey out. Of course there would be no introduction since Clark Oliver was already acquainted with the lady. I was wondering how I was to locate her when I got a shock that made me dizzy. Jane was over in a corner looking at me.

There was no time to collect my wits. The guests were moving out to the dining-room. I took my nerve in my hand, crossed the room, bowed, and the next moment was walking through the hall with Jane's hand on my arm. The hall was a good long one; I blessed the architect who had planned it. It gave me time to sort out my ideas.

Jane here! Jane going out to dinner with me, believing me to be Clark Oliver! Jane — but it was incredible! The whole thing was a dream — or I had gone crazy!

I looked at her sideways when we had got into our places at the table. She was more beautiful than ever, that tall, brown-haired, disdainful Jane. The settlement work story I was inclined to dismiss as a myth. Settlement work in a beautiful woman generally means crowsfeet or a broken heart. Jane, according to my sight and belief, possessed neither.

Once upon a time I had been engaged to Jane. I had been idiotically in love with her in those days and still more idiotically believed that she loved me. The trouble was that, although I had been cured of the latter phase of my idiocy, the former had become chronic. I had never been able to get over loving Jane. All through those two years I had hugged the fond hope that sometime I might stumble across her in a mild mood and make matters up. There was no such thing as seeking her out or writing to her, since she had icily forbidden me to do so, and Jane had a most detestable habit — in a woman — of meaning what she said. But the deity I had invoked was the god of chance — and this was how he had answered my prayers. I was eating my dinner beside Jane, who supposed me to be Clark Oliver!

What should I do? Confess the truth and plead my cause while she had to sit beside me? That would never do. Someone might overhear us. And, in any case, it would be no passport to Jane's favor that I was a guest in the house under false pretences. She would be certain to disapprove strongly. It was a maddening situation.

Jane, who was calmly eating soup — she was the only woman I had ever seen who could eat soup and look like a

119

goddess at the same time — glanced around and caught me studying her profile. I thought she blushed slightly and I raged inwardly to think that blush was meant for Clark Oliver — Clark Oliver who had told me he thought Jane was smitten on him! Jane! On him!

"Do you know, Mr. Oliver," said Jane slowly, "that you are startlingly like a—a person I used to know? When I first saw you the other night I took you for him."

A *person* you used to know! Oh, Jane, that was the most unkindest cut of all.

"My cousin, Elliott Cameron, I suppose?" I answered as indifferently as I could. "We resemble each other very closely. You were acquainted with Cameron, Miss Harvey?"

"Slightly," said Jane.

"A fine fellow," I said unblushingly.

"A-h," said Jane.

"My favorite relative," I went on brazenly. "He's a thoroughly good sort — rather dull now to what he used to be, though. He had an unfortunate love affair two years ago and has never got over it."

"Indeed?" said Jane coldly, crumbling a bit of bread between her fingers. Her face was expressionless and her voice ditto; but I had heard her criticize nervous people who did things like that at table.

"I fear poor Elliott's life has been completely spoiled," I said, with a sigh. "It's a shame."

"Did he confide the affair to you?" asked Jane, a little scornfully.

"Well, after a fashion. He said enough for me to guess the rest. He never told me the lady's name. She was very beautiful, I understand, and very heartless. Oh, she used him very badly."

"Did he tell you that, too?" asked Jane.

"Not he. He won't listen to a word against her. But a chap can draw his own conclusions, you know."

"What went wrong between them?" asked Jane. She smiled at a lady across the table, as if she were merely asking questions to make conversation, but she went on crumbling bread.

"Simply a very stiff quarrel, I believe. Elliott never went into details. The lady was flirting with somebody else, I fancy."

"People have such different ideas about flirting," said Jane, languidly. "What one would call mere simple friendliness another construes into flirting. Possibly your friend — or is it your cousin? — is one of those men who become insanely jealous over every trifle and attempt to exert authority before they have any to exert. A woman of spirit would hardly fail to resent that."

"Of course Elliott was jealous," I admitted. "But then, you know, Miss Harvey, that jealousy is said to be the measure of a man's love. If he went beyond his rights I am sure he is bitterly sorry for it."

"Does he really care about her still?" asked Jane, eating most industriously, although somehow the contents of her plate did not grow noticeably less. As for me, I didn't pretend to eat. I simply pecked.

"He loves her with all his heart," I answered fervently. "There never has been and never will be any other woman for Elliott Cameron."

"Why doesn't he go and tell her so?" inquired Jane, as if she felt rather bored over the whole subject.

"He doesn't dare to. She forbade him ever to cross her path again. Told him she hated him and always would hate him as long as she lived."

"She must have been an unpleasantly emphatic young woman," commented Jane.

"I'd like to hear anyone say so to Elliott," I responded. "He considers her perfection. I'm sorry for Elliott. His life is wrecked."

"Do you know," said Jane slowly, as if poking about in the recesses of her memory for something half forgotten. "I believe I know the—the girl in question."

"Really?" I said.

"Yes, she is a friend of mine. She—she never told me his name, but putting two and two together, I believe it must have been your cousin. But she—she thinks she was the one to blame."

"Does she?" It was my turn to ask questions now, but my heart thumped so that I could hardly speak.

"Yes, she says she was too hasty and unreasonable. She didn't mean to flirt at all — and she never cared for anyone but—him. But his jealousy irritated her. I suppose she said things to him she didn't really mean. She—she never supposed he was going to take her at her word."

"Do you think she cares for him still?" Considering what was at stake, I think I asked the question very well.

"I think she must," said Jane languidly. "She has never looked at any other man. She devotes most of her time to charitable work, but I feel sure she isn't really happy."

So the settlement story was true. Oh, Jane!

"What would you advise my cousin to do?" I asked. "Do you think he should go boldly to her? Would she listen to him — forgive him?"

"She might," said Jane.

"Have I your permission to tell Elliott Cameron this?" I demanded.

Jane selected and ate an olive with maddening deliberation.

"I suppose you may — if you are really convinced that he wants to hear it," she said at last, as if barely recollecting that I had asked the question two minutes previously.

"I'll tell him as soon as I go home," I said.

I had the satisfaction of startling Jane at last. She turned her head and looked at me. I got a good, square, satisfying gaze into her big, blackish-blue eyes.

"Yes," I said, compelling myself to look away. "He came in on the boat this afternoon too late for his train. Has to stay over till to-morrow night. I left him in my rooms when I came away. Doubtless to-morrow will see him speeding recklessly to his dear divinity. I wonder if he knows where she is at present."

"If he doesn't," said Jane, with the air of dismissing the subject once and forever from her mind, "I can give him the information. You may tell him I'm staying with the Duncan Moores, and shall be leaving day after to-morrow. By the way, have you seen Mrs. Kennedy's collection of steins? It is a remarkably fine one."

Clark Oliver couldn't come to our wedding — or wouldn't. Jane has never met him since, but she cannot understand why I have such an aversion to him, especially when he has such a good opinion of me. She says she thought him charming, and one of the most interesting conversationalists she ever went out to dinner with.

Abel and His Great Adventure

"Come out of doors, master — come out of doors. I can't talk or think right with walls around me — never could. Let's go out to the garden." These were almost the first words I ever heard Abel Armstrong say. He was a member of the board of school trustees in Stillwater, and I had not met him before this late May evening, when I had gone down to confer with him upon some small matter of business. For I was "the new schoolmaster" in Stillwater, having taken the school for the summer term.

It was a rather lonely country district — a fact of which I was glad, for life had been going somewhat awry with me and my heart was sore and rebellious over many things that have nothing to do with this narration. Stillwater offered time and opportunity for healing and counsel. Yet, looking back, I doubt if I should have found either had it not been for Abel and his beloved garden.

Abel Armstrong (he was always called "Old Abel", though he was barely sixty) lived in a quaint, gray house close by the harbour shore. I heard a good deal about him before I saw him. He was called "queer", but Stillwater folks seemed to be very fond of him. He and his sister, Tamzine, lived together; she, so my garrulous landlady informed me, had not been sound of mind at times for many years; but she was all right now, only odd and quiet. Abel had gone to college for a year when he was young, but had given it up when Tamzine "went crazy". There was no one else to look after her. Abel had settled down to it with apparent content: at least he had never complained.

"Always took things easy, Abel did," said Mrs. Campbell.

"Never seemed to worry over disappointments and trials as most folks do. Seems to me that as long as Abel Armstrong can stride up and down in that garden of his, reciting poetry and speeches, or talking to that yaller cat of his as if it was a human, he doesn't care much how the world wags on. He never had much git-up-and-git. His father was a hustler, but the family didn't take after him. They all favoured the mother's people — sorter shiftless and dreamy. 'Taint the way to git on in this world."

No, good and worthy Mrs. Campbell. It was not the way to get on in your world; but there are other worlds where getting on is estimated by different standards, and Abel Armstrong lived in one of these — a world far beyond the ken of the thrifty Stillwater farmers and fishers. Something of this I had sensed, even before I saw him; and that night in his garden, under a sky of smoky red, blossoming into stars above the harbour, I found a friend whose personality and philosophy were to calm and harmonize and enrich my whole existence. This sketch is my grateful tribute to one of the rarest and finest souls God ever clothed with clay.

He was a tall man, somewhat ungainly of figure and homely of face. But his large, deep eyes of velvety nut-brown were very beautiful and marvellously bright and clear for a man of his age. He wore a little pointed, well-cared-for beard, innocent of gray; but his hair was grizzled, and altogether he had the appearance of a man who had passed through many sorrows which had marked his body as well as his soul. Looking at him, I doubted Mrs. Campbell's conclusion that he had not "minded" giving up college. This man had given up much and felt it deeply; but he had outlived the pain and the blessing of sacrifice had come to him. His voice was very melodious and beautiful, and the brown hand he held out to me was peculiarly long and shapely and flexible.

We went out to the garden in the scented moist air of a maritime spring evening. Behind the garden was a cloudy pine wood; the house closed it in on the left, while in front and on the right a row of tall Lombardy poplars stood out in stately purple silhouette against the sunset sky.

"Always liked Lombardies," said Abel, waving a long arm at them. "They are the trees of princesses. When I was a boy they were fashionable. Anyone who had any pretensions to gentility had a row of Lombardies at the foot of his lawn or up his lane, or at any rate one on either side of his front door. They're out of fashion now. Folks complain they die at the top and get ragged-looking. So they do — so they do, if you don't risk your neck every spring climbing up a light ladder to trim them out as I do. My neck isn't worth much to anyone, which, I suppose, is why I've never broken it; and *my* Lombardies never look out-at-elbows. My mother was especially fond of them. She liked their dignity and their stand-offishness. *They* don't hobnob with every Tom, Dick and Harry. If it's pines for company, master, it's Lombardies for society."

We stepped from the front doorstone into the garden. There was another entrance — a sagging gate flanked by two branching white lilacs. From it a little dappled path led to a huge apple-tree in the centre, a great swelling cone of rosy blossom with a mossy circular seat around its trunk. But Abel's favourite seat, so he told me, was lower down the slope, under a little trellis overhung with the delicate emerald of young hop-vines. He led me to it and pointed proudly to the fine view of the harbour visible from it. The early sunset glow of rose and flame had faded out of the sky; the water was silvery and mirror-like; dim sails drifted along by the darkening shore. A bell was ringing in a small Catholic chapel across the harbour. Mellowly and dreamily sweet the chime floated through the dusk, blent with the moan of the sea. The great revolving light at the channel trembled and flashed against the opal sky, and far out, beyond the golden sand-dunes of the bar, was the crinkled gray ribbon of a passing steamer's smoke.

"There, isn't that view worth looking at?" said old Abel,

126

with a loving, proprietary pride. "You don't have to pay anything for it, either. All that sea and sky free — 'without money and without price'. Let's sit down here in the hop-vine arbour, master. There'll be a moonrise presently. I'm never tired of finding out what a moonrise sheen can be like over that sea. There's a surprise in it every time. Now, master, you're getting your mouth in the proper shape to talk business — but don't you do it. Nobody should talk business when he's expecting a moonrise. Not that I like talking business at any time."

"Unfortunately it has to be talked of sometimes, Mr. Armstrong," I said.

"Yes, it seems to be a necessary evil, master," he acknowledged. "But I know what business you've come upon, and we can settle it in five minutes after the moon's well up. I'll just agree to everything you and the other two trustees want. Lord knows why they ever put *me* on the school board. Maybe it's because I'm so ornamental. They wanted one good-looking man, I reckon."

His low chuckle, so full of mirth and so free from malice, was infectious. I laughed also, as I sat down in the hop-vine arbour.

"Now, you needn't talk if you don't want to," he said. "And I won't. We'll just sit here, sociable like, and if we think of anything worth while to say we'll say it. Otherwise, not. If you can sit in silence with a person for half an hour and feel comfortable, you and that person can be friends. If you can't, friends you'll never be, and you needn't waste time in trying."

Abel and I passed successfully the test of silence that evening in the hop-vine arbour. I was strangely content to sit and think — something I had not cared to do lately. A peace, long unknown to my stormy soul, seemed hovering near it. The garden was steeped in it; old Abel's personality radiated it. I looked about me and wondered whence came the charm of that tangled, unworldly spot.

"Nice and far from the market-place isn't it?" asked Abel

suddenly, as if he had heard my unasked question. "No buying and selling and getting gain here. Nothing was ever sold out of *this* garden. Tamzine has her vegetable plot over yonder, but what we don't eat we give away. Geordie Marr down the harbour has a big garden like this and he sells heaps of flowers and fruit and vegetables to the hotel folks. He thinks I'm an awful fool because I won't do the same. Well, he gets money out of his garden and I get happiness out of mine. That's the difference. S'posing I could make more money — what then? I'd only be taking it from people that needed it more. There's enough for Tamzine and me. As for Geordie Marr, there isn't a more unhappy creature on God's earth — he's always stewing in a broth of trouble, poor man. O' course, he brews up most of it for himself, but I reckon that doesn't make it any easier to bear. Ever sit in a hop-vine arbour before, master?"

I was to grow used to Abel's abrupt change of subject. I answered that I never had.

"Great place for dreaming," said Abel complacently. "Being young, no doubt, you dream a-plenty."

I answered hotly and bitterly that I had done with dreams.

"No, you haven't," said Abel meditatively. "You may *think* you have. What then? First thing you know you'll be dreaming again — thank the Lord for it. I ain't going to ask you what's soured you on dreaming just now. After awhile you'll begin again, especially if you come to this garden as much as I hope you will. It's chockful of dreams — *any* kind of dreams. You take your choice. Now, *I* favour dreams of adventures, if you'll believe it. I'm sixty-one and I never do anything rasher than go out cod-fishing on a fine day, but I still lust after adventures. Then I dream I'm an awful fellow — blood-thirsty."

I burst out laughing. Perhaps laughter was somewhat rare in that old garden. Tamzine, who was weeding at the far end, lifted her head in a startled fashion and walked past us into the house. She did not look at us or speak to us. She was reputed to be abnormally shy. She was very stout and wore a dress of bright red-and-white striped material. Her face was round and blank, but her reddish hair was abundant and beautiful. A huge, orange-coloured cat was at her heels; as she passed us he bounded over to the arbour and sprang up on Abel's knee. He was a gorgeous brute, with vivid green eyes, and immense white double paws.

"Captain Kidd, Mr. Woodley." He introduced us as seriously as if the cat had been a human being. Neither Captain Kidd nor I responded very enthusiastically.

"You don't like cats, I reckon, master," said Abel, stroking the Captain's velvet back. "I don't blame you. I was never fond of them myself until I found the Captain. I saved his life and when you've saved a creature's life you're bound to love it. It's next thing to giving it life. There are some terrible thoughtless people in the world, master. Some of those city folks who have summer homes down the harbour are so thoughtless that they're cruel. It's the worst kind of cruelty, I think — the thoughtless kind. You can't cope with it. They keep cats there in the summer and feed them and pet them and doll them up with ribbons and collars; and then in the fall they go off and leave them to starve or freeze. It makes my blood boil, master."

"One day last winter I found a poor old mother cat dead on the shore, lying against the skin and bone bodies of her three little kittens. She had died trying to shelter them. She had her poor stiff claws around them. Master, I cried. Then I swore. Then I carried those poor little kittens home and fed 'hem up and found good homes for them. I know the woman who left the cat. When she comes back this summer I'm going to go down and tell her my opinion of her. It'll be rank meddling, but, lord, how I love meddling in a good cause."

"Was Captain Kidd one of the forsaken?" I asked.

"Yes. I found him one bitter cold day in winter caught

in the branches of a tree by his darn-fool ribbon collar. He was almost starving. Lord, if you could have seen his eyes! He was nothing but a kitten, and he'd got his living somehow since he'd been left till he got hung up. When I loosed him he gave my hand a pitiful swipe with his little red tongue. He wasn't the prosperous free-booter you behold now. He was meek as Moses. That was nine years ago. His life has been long in the land for a cat. He's a good old pal, the Captain is."

"I should have expected you to have a dog," I said.

Abel shook his head.

"I had a dog once. I cared so much for him that when he died I couldn't bear the thought of ever getting another in his place. He was a *friend* — you understand? The Captain's only a pal. I'm fond of the Captain — all the fonder because of the spice of deviltry there is in all cats. But I *loved* my dog. There isn't any devil in a good dog. That's why they're more lovable than cats — but I'm darned if they're as interesting.

I laughed as I rose regretfully.

"Must you go, master? And we haven't talked any business after all. I reckon it's that stove matter you've come about. It's like those two fool trustees to start up a stove sputter in spring. It's a wonder they didn't leave it till dog-days and begin then."

"They merely wished me to ask you if you approved of putting in a new stove."

"Tell them to put in a new stove — any kind of a new stove — and be hanged to them," rejoined Abel. "As for you, master, you're welcome to this garden any time. If you're tired or lonely, or too ambitious or angry, come here and sit awhile, master. Do you think any man could keep mad if he sat and looked into the heart of a pansy for ten minutes? When you feel like talking, I'll talk, and when you feel like thinking, I'll let you. I'm a great hand to leave folks alone."

"I think I'll come often," I said, "perhaps too often."

"Not likely, master — not likely — not after we've watched a moonrise contentedly together. It's as good a test of compatibility as any I know. You're young and I'm old, but our souls are about the same age, I reckon, and we'll find lots to say to each other. Are you going straight home from here?"

"Yes."

"Then I'm going to bother you to stop for a moment at Mary Bascom's and give her a bouquet of my white lilacs. She loves 'em and I'm not going to wait till she's dead to send her flowers."

"She's very ill just now, isn't she?"

"She's got the Bascom consumption. That means she may die in a month, like her brother, or linger on for twenty years, like her father. But long or short, white lilac in spring is sweet, and I'm sending her a fresh bunch every day while it lasts. It's a rare night, master. I envy you your walk home in the moonlight along that shore."

"Better come part of the way with me," I suggested.

"No." Abel glanced at the house. "Tamzine never likes to be alone o' nights. So I take my moonlight walks in the garden. The moon's a great friend of mine, master. I've loved her ever since I can remember. When I was a little lad of eight I fell asleep in the garden one evening and wasn't missed. I woke up alone in the night and I was most scared to death, master. Lord, what shadows and queer noises there were! I darsn't move. I just sat there quaking, poor small mite. Then all at once I saw the moon looking down at me through the pine boughs, just like an old friend. I was comforted right off. Got up and walked to the house as brave as a lion, looking at her. Goodnight, master. Tell Mary the lilacs 'll last another week yet."

From that night Abel and I were cronies. We walked and talked and kept silence and fished cod together. Stillwater people thought it very strange that I should prefer his society to that of the young fellows of my own age. Mrs. Campbell was quite worried over it, and opined that there had always been something queer about me. "Birds of a feather."

I loved that old garden by the harbour shore. Even Abel himself, I think, could hardly have felt a deeper affection for it. When its gate closed behind me it shut out the world and my corroding memories and discontents. In its peace my soul emptied itself of the bitterness which had been filling and spoiling it, and grew normal and healthy again, aided thereto by Abel's wise words. He never preached, but he radiated courage and endurance and a frank acceptance of the hard things of life, as well as a cordial welcome of its pleasant things. He was the *sanest* soul I ever met. He neither minimized ill nor exaggerated good, but he held that we should never be controlled by either. Pain should not depress us unduly, nor pleasure lure us into forgetfulness and sloth. All unknowingly he made me realize that I had been a bit of a coward and a shirker. I began to understand that my personal woes were not the most important things in the universe, even to myself. In short, Abel taught me to laugh again; and when a man can laugh wholesomely things are not going too badly with him.

That old garden was always such a cheery place. Even when the east wind sang in minor and the waves on the gray shore were sad, hints of sunshine seemed to be lurking all about it. Perhaps this was because there were so many yellow flowers in it. Tamzine liked yellow flowers. Captain Kidd, too, always paraded it in panoply of gold. He was so large and effulgent that one hardly missed the sun. Considering his presence I wondered that the garden was always so full of singing birds. But the Captain never meddled with them. Probably he understood that his master would not have tolerated it for a moment. So there was always a song or a chirp somewhere. Overhead flew the gulls and the cranes. The wind in the pines always made a glad salutation. Abel and I paced the walks, [in] high converse on matters beyond the ken of cat or king.

"I liked to ponder on all problems, though I can never solve them," Abel used to say. "My father held that we should never talk of things we couldn't understand. But, lord, master, if we didn't the subjects for conversation would be mighty few. I reckon the gods laugh many a time to hear us, but what matter? So long as we remember that we're only men, and don't take to fancying ourselves gods, really knowing good and evil. I reckon our discussions won't do us or anyone much harm. So we'll have another whack at the origin of evil this evening, master."

Tamzine forgot to be shy with me at last, and gave me a broad smile of welcome every time I came. But she rarely spoke to me. She spent all her spare time weeding the garden, which she loved as well as Abel did. She was addicted to bright colours and always wore wrappers of very gorgeous print. She worshipped Abel and his word was a law unto her.

"I am very thankful Tamzine is so well," said Abel one evening as we watched the sunset. The day had begun sombrely in gray cloud and mist, but it ended in a pomp of scarlet and gold. "There was a time when she wasn't, master — you've heard? But for years now she has been quite able to look after herself. And so, if I fare forth on the last great adventure some of these days Tamzine will not be left helpless."

"She is ten years older than you. It is likely she will go before you," I said.

Abel shook his head and stroked his smart beard. I always suspected that beard of being Abel's last surviving vanity. It was always so carefully groomed, while I had no evidence that he ever combed his grizzled mop of hair.

"No, Tamzine will outlive me. She's got the Armstrong heart. I have the Marwood heart — my mother was a Marwood. We don't live to be old, and we go quick and easy. I'm glad of it. I don't think I'm a coward, master, but the thought of a lingering death gives me a queer sick feeling of horror. There, I'm not going to say any more about it. I just mentioned it so that some day when you hear that old Abel Armstrong has been found dead, you won't feel sorry. You'll remember I wanted it that way. Not that I'm tired of life either. It's very pleasant, what with my garden and Captain Kidd and the harbour out there. But it's a trifle monotonous at times and death will be something of a change, master. I'm real curious about it."

"I hate the thought of death," I said gloomily.

"Oh, you're young. The young always do. Death grows friendlier as we grow older. Not that one of us really wants to die, though, master. Tennyson spoke truth when he said that. There's old Mrs. Warner at the Channel Head. She's had heaps of trouble all her life, poor soul, and she's lost almost everyone she cared about. She's always saying that she'll be glad when her time comes, and she doesn't want to live any longer in this vale of tears. But when she takes a sick spell, lord, what a fuss she makes, master! Doctors from town and a trained nurse and enough medicine to kill a dog! Life may be a vale of tears, all right, master, but there are some folks who enjoy weeping, I reckon."

Summer passed through the garden with her procession of roses and lilies and hollyhocks and golden glow. The golden glow was particularly fine that year. There was a great bank of it at the lower end of the garden, like a huge billow of sunshine. Tamzine revelled in it, but Abel liked more subtly-tinted flowers. There was a certain dark wine-hued hollyhock which was a favourite with him. He would sit for hours looking steadfastly into one of its shallow satin cups. I found him so one afternoon in the hop-vine arbour.

"This colour always has a soothing effect on me," he explained. "Yellow excites me too much — makes me rest-less — makes me want to sail 'beyond the bourne of sunset'. I looked at that surge of golden glow down there today till I got all worked up and thought my life had been an awful failure. I found a dead butterfly and had a little funeral — buried it in the fern corner. And I thought I hadn't been any more use in the world than that poor little butterfly. Oh, I was woeful, master. Then I got me this hollyhock and sat down here to look at it alone. When a man's alone, master, he's most with God — or with the devil. The devil rampaged around me all the time I was looking at that golden glow; but God spoke to me through the hollyhock. And it seemed to me that a man who's as happy as I am and has got such a garden has made a real success of living."

"I hope I'll be able to make as much of a success," I said sincerely.

"I want you to make a different kind of success, though, master," said Abel, shaking his head. "I want you to *do* things — the things I'd have tried to do if I'd had the chance. It's in you to do them — if you set your teeth and go ahead."

"I believe I *can* set my teeth and go ahead now, thanks to you, Mr. Armstrong," I said. "I was heading straight for failure when I came here last spring; but you've changed my course."

"Given you a sort of compass to steer by, haven't I?" queried Abel with a smile. "I ain't too modest to take some credit for it. I saw I could do *you* some good. But my garden has done more than I did, if you'll believe it. It's wonderful what a garden can do for a man when he lets it have its way. Come, sit down here and bask, master. The sunshine may be gone to-morrow. Let's just sit and think."

We sat and thought for a long while. Presently Abel said abruptly:

"You don't see the folks I see in this garden, master. You don't see anybody but me and old Tamzine and Captain Kidd. I see all who used to be here long ago. It was a lively place then. There were plenty of us and we were as gay a set of youngsters as you'd find anywhere. We tossed laughter backwards and forwards here like a ball. And now old Tamzine and older Abel are all that are left."

He was silent a moment, looking at the phantoms of memory that paced invisibly to me the dappled walks and peeped merrily through the swinging boughs. Then he went on:

"Of all the folks I see here there are two that are more vivid and real than all the rest, master. One is my sister Alice. She died thirty years ago. She was very beautiful. You'd hardly believe that to look at Tamzine and me, would you? But it is true. We always called her Queen Alice — she was so stately and handsome. She had brown eyes and red gold hair, just the colour of that nasturtium there. She was father's favourite. The night she was born they didn't think my mother would live. Father walked this garden all night. And just under that old apple-tree he knelt at sunrise and thanked God when they came to tell him that all was well.

"Alice was always a creature of joy. This old garden rang with her laughter in those years. She seldom walked — she ran or danced. She only lived twenty years, but nineteen of them were so happy I've never pitied her over much. She had everything that makes life worth living — laughter and love, and at the last sorrow. James Milburn was her lover. It's thirty-one years since his ship sailed out of that harbour and Alice waved him good-bye from this garden. He never came back. His ship was never heard of again.

"When Alice gave up hope that it would be, she died of a broken heart. They say there's no such thing; but nothing else ailed Alice. She stood at yonder gate day after day and watched the harbour; and when at last she gave up hope life went with it. I remember the day: she had watched until sunset. Then she turned away from the gate. All the unrest and despair had gone out of her eyes. There was a terrible peace in them — the peace of the dead. 'He will never come back now, Abel,' she said to me.

"In less than a week she was dead. The others mourned her, but I didn't, master. She had sounded the deeps of living and there was nothing else to linger through the years for. *My* grief had spent itself earlier, when I walked

136

this garden in agony because I could not help her. But often, on these long warm summer afternoons, I seem to hear Alice's laughter all over this garden; though she's been dead so long."

He lapsed into a reverie which I did not disturb, and it was not until another day that I learned of the other memory that he cherished. He reverted to it suddenly as we sat again in the hop-vine arbour, looking at the glimmering radiance of the September sea.

"Master, how many of us are sitting here?"

"Two in the flesh. How many in the spirit I know not," I answered, humouring his mood.

"There is one — the other of the two I spoke of the day I told you about Alice. It's harder for me to speak of this one."

"Don't speak of it if it hurts you," I said.

"But I want to. It's a whim of mine. Do you know why I told you of Alice and why I'm going to tell you of Mercedes? It's because I want someone to remember them and think of them sometimes after I'm gone. I can't bear that their names should be utterly forgotten by all living souls.

"My older brother, Alec, was a sailor, and on his last voyage to the West Indies he married and brought home a Spanish girl. My father and mother didn't like the match. Mercedes was a foreigner and a Catholic, and differed from us in every way. But I never blamed Alec after I saw her. It wasn't that she was so very pretty. She was slight and dark and ivory-coloured. But she was very graceful, and there was a charm about her, master — a mighty and potent charm. The women couldn't understand it. They wondered at Alec's infatuation for her. I never did. I—I loved her, too, master, before I had known her a day. Nobody ever knew it. Mercedes never dreamed of it. But it's lasted me all my life. I never wanted to think of any other woman. She spoiled a man for any other kind of woman — that little pale, dark-eyed Spanish girl. To love

137

her was like drinking some rare sparkling wine. You'd never again have any taste for a commoner draught.

"I think she was very happy the year she spent here. Our thrifty women-folk in Stillwater jeered at her because she wasn't what they called capable. They said she couldn't do anything. But she could do one thing well — she could love. She worshipped Alec. I used to hate him for it. Oh, my heart has been very full of black thoughts in its time, master. But neither Alec nor Mercedes ever knew. And I'm thankful now that they were so happy. Alec made this arbour for Mercedes — at least he made the trellis, and she planted the vines.

"She used to sit here most of the time in summer. I suppose that's why I like to sit here. Her eyes would be dreamy and far-away until Alec would flash his welcome. How that used to torture me! But now I like to remember it. And her pretty soft foreign voice and little white hands. She died after she had lived here a year. They buried her and her baby in the graveyard of that little chapel over the harbour where the bell rings every evening. She used to like sitting here and listening to it. Alec lived a long while after, but he never married again. He's gone now, and nobody remembers Mercedes but me."

Abel lapsed into a reverie — a tryst with the past which I would not disturb. I thought he did not notice my departure, but as I opened the gate he stood up and waved his hand.

Three days later I went again to the old garden by the harbour shore. There was a red light on a distant sail. In the far west a sunset city was built around a great deep harbour of twilight. Palaces were there and bannered towers of crimson and gold. The air was full of music; there was one music of the wind and another of the waves, and still another of the distant bell from the chapel near which Mercedes slept. The garden was full of ripe odours and warm colours. The Lombardies around it were tall and sombre like the priestly forms of some mystic band.

Abel was sitting in the hop-vine arbour; beside him Captain Kidd slept. I thought Abel was asleep, too; his head leaned against the trellis and his eyes were shut.

But when I reached the arbour I saw that he was not asleep. There was a strange, wise little smile on his lips as if he had attained to the ultimate wisdom and were laughing in no unkindly fashion at our old blind suppositions and perplexities.

Abel had gone on his Great Adventure.

The Garden of Spices

Jims tried the door of the blue room. Yes, it was locked. He had hoped Aunt Augusta *might* have forgotten to lock it; but when did Aunt Augusta forget anything? Except, perhaps, that little boys were not born grown-ups — and *that* was something she never remembered. To be sure, she was only a half-aunt. Whole aunts probably had more convenient memories.

Jims turned and stood with his back against the door. It was better that way; he could not imagine things behind him then. And the blue room was so big and dim that a dreadful number of things could be imagined in it. All the windows were shuttered but one, and that one was so darkened by a big pine tree branching right across it that it did not let in much light.

Jims looked very small and lost and lonely as he shrank back against the door — so small and lonely that one might have thought that even the sternest of half-aunts should have thought twice before shutting him up in that room and telling him he must stay there the whole afternoon instead of going out for a promised ride. Jims hated being shut up alone — especially in the blue room. Its bigness and dimness and silence filled his sensitive little soul with vague horror. Sometimes he became almost sick with fear in it. To do Aunt Augusta justice, she never suspected this. If she had she would not have decreed this particular punishment, because she knew Jims was delicate and must not be subjected to any great physical or mental strain. That was why she shut him up instead of whipping him. But how was she to know it? Aunt Augusta was one of those people who never know anything unless it is told them in plain language and then hammered into their heads. There was no one to tell her but Jims, and Jims would have died the death before he would have told Aunt Augusta, with her cold, spectacled eyes and thin, smileless mouth, that he was desperately frightened when he was shut in the blue room. So he was always shut in it for punishment; and the punishments came very often, for Jims was always doing things that Aunt Augusta considered naughty. At first, this time, Jims did not feel quite so frightened as usual because he was very angry. As he put it, he was very mad at Aunt Augusta. He hadn't *meant* to spill his pudding over the floor and the tablecloth and his clothes; and how such a little bit of pudding — Aunt Augusta was mean with desserts — could ever have spread itself over so much territory Jims could not understand. But he had made a terrible mess and Aunt Augusta had been very angry and had said he must be cured of such carelessness. She said he must spend the afternoon in the blue room instead of going for a ride with Mrs. Loring in her new car.

Jims was bitterly disappointed. If Uncle Walter had been home Jims would have appealed to him — for when Uncle Walter could be really wakened up to a realization of his small nephew's presence in his home, he was very kind and indulgent. But it was so hard to waken him up that Jims seldom attempted it. He liked Uncle Walter, but as far as being acquainted with him went he might as well have been the inhabitant of a star in the Milky Way. Jims was just a lonely, solitary little creature, and sometimes he felt so friendless that his eyes smarted, and several sobs had to be swallowed.

There were no sobs just now, though — Jims was still too angry. It wasn't fair. It was so seldom he got a car ride. Uncle Walter was always too busy, attending to sick children all over the town, to take him. It was only once in a blue moon Mrs. Loring asked him to go out with her.

141

But she always ended up with ice cream or a movie, and to-day Jims had had strong hopes that both were on the programme.

"I hate Aunt Augusta," he said aloud; and then the sound of his voice in that huge, still room scared him so that he only thought the rest. "I won't have any fun — and she won't feed my gobbler, either."

Jims had shrieked "Feed my gobbler," to the old servant as he had been hauled upstairs. But he didn't think Nancy Jane had heard him, and nobody, not even Jims, could imagine Aunt Augusta feeding the gobbler. It was always a wonder to him that she ate, herself. It seemed really too human a thing for her to do.

"I wish I had spilled that pudding *on purpose*," Jims said vindictively, and with the saying his anger evaporated — Jims never could stay angry long — and left him merely a scared little fellow, with velvety, nut-brown eyes full of fear that should have no place in a child's eyes. He looked so small and helpless as he crouched against the door that one might have wondered if even Aunt Augusta would not have relented had she seen him.

How that window at the far end of the room rattled! It sounded terribly as if somebody — or *something* — were trying to get in. Jims looked desperately at the unshuttered window. He must get to it; once there, he could curl up in the window seat, his back to the wall, and forget the shadows by looking out into the sunshine and loveliness of the garden over the wall. Jims would have likely have been found dead of fright in that blue room some time had it not been for the garden over the wall.

But to get to the window Jims must cross the room and pass by the bed. Jims held that bed in special dread. It was the oldest fashioned thing in the old-fashioned, old-furnitured house. It was high and rigid, and hung with gloomy blue curtains. *Anything* might jump out of such a bed.

Jims gave a gasp and ran madly across the room. He reached the window and flung himself upon the seat. With a sigh of relief he curled down in the corner. Outside, over the high brick wall, was a world where his imagination could roam, though his slender little body was pent a prisoner in the blue room.

Jims had loved that garden from his first sight of it. He called it the Garden of Spices and wove all sorts of yarns in fancy — yarns gay and tragic — about it. He had only known it for a few weeks. Before that, they had lived in a much smaller house away at the other side of the town. Then Uncle Walter's uncle — who had brought him up just as he was bringing up Jims — had died, and they had all come to live in Uncle Walter's old home. Somehow, Jims had an idea that Uncle Walter wasn't very glad to come back there. But he had to, according to great-uncle's will. Jims himself didn't mind much. He liked the smaller rooms in their former home better, but the Garden of Spices made up for all.

It was such a beautiful spot. Just inside the wall was a row of aspen poplars that always talked in silvery whispers and shook their dainty, heart-shaped leaves at him. Beyond them, under scattered pines, was a rockery where ferns and wild things grew. It was almost as good as a bit of woods — and Jims loved the woods, though he scarcely ever saw them. Then, past the pines, were roses just breaking into June bloom — roses in such profusion as Jims hadn't known existed, with dear little paths twisting about among the bushes. It seemed to be a garden where no frost could blight or rough wind blow. When rain fell it must fall very gently. Past the roses one saw a green lawn, sprinkled over now with the white ghosts of dandelions, and dotted with ornamental trees. The trees grew so thickly that they almost hid the house to which the garden pertained. It was a large one of grey-black stone, with stacks of huge chimneys. Jims had no idea who lived there. He had asked Aunt Augusta and Aunt Augusta had frowned and told him it did not matter who lived there and that he must never, on any account, mention the next house or its occupant to Uncle Walter. Jims would never have thought of mentioning them to Uncle Walter. But the prohibition filled him with an unholy and unsubduable curiosity. He was devoured by the desire to find out who the folks in that tabooed house were.

And he longed to have the freedom of that garden. Jims loved gardens. There had been a garden at the little house but there was none here — nothing but an old lawn that had been fine once but was now badly run to seed. Jims had heard Uncle Walter say that he was going to have it attended to but nothing had been done yet. And meanwhile here was a beautiful garden over the wall which looked as if it should be full of children. But no children were ever in it — or anybody else apparently. And so, in spite of its beauty, it had a lonely look that hurt Jims. He *wanted* his Garden of Spices to be full of laughter. He pictured himself running in it with imaginary playmates — and there was a mother in it — or a big sister — or, at the least, a whole aunt who would let you hug her and would never dream of shutting you up in chilly, shadowy, horrible blue rooms.

"It seems to me," said Jims, flattening his nose against the pane, "that I must get into that garden or bust."

Aunt Augusta would have said icily, "We do not use such expressions, James," but Aunt Augusta was not there to hear.

"I'm afraid the Very Handsome Cat isn't coming to-day," sighed Jims. Then he brightened up; the Very Handsome Cat was coming across the lawn. He was the only living thing, barring birds and butterflies, that Jims ever saw in the garden. Jims worshipped that cat. He was jet black, with white paws and dickey, and he had as much dignity as ten cats. Jims' fingers tingled to stroke him. Jims had never been allowed to have even a kitten because Aunt Augusta had a horror of cats. And you cannot stroke gobblers!

The Very Handsome Cat came through the rose garden

paths on his beautiful paws, ambled daintily around the rockery, and sat down in a shady spot under a pine tree, right where Jims could see him, through a gap in the little poplars. He looked straight up at Jims and winked. At least, Jims always believed and declared he did. And that wink said, or seemed to say, plainly:

"Be a sport. Come down here and play with me. A fig for your Aunt Augusta!"

A wild, daring, absurd idea flashed into Jims' brain. Could he? He could! He would! He knew it would be easy. He had thought it all out many times, although until now he had never dreamed of really doing it. To unhook the window and swing it open, to step out on the pine bough and from it to another that hung over the wall and dropped nearly to the ground, to spring from it to the velvet sward under the poplars — why, it was all the work of a minute. With a careful, repressed whoop Jims ran towards the Very Handsome Cat.

The cat rose and retreated in deliberate haste; Jims ran after him. The cat dodged through the rose paths and eluded Jims' eager hands, just keeping tantalizingly out of reach. Jims had forgotten everything except that he must catch the cat. He was full of a fearful joy, with an elfin delight running through it. He had escaped from the blue room and its ghosts; he was in his Garden of Spices; he had got the better of mean old Aunt Augusta. But he *must* catch the cat.

The cat ran over the lawn and Jims pursued it through the green gloom of the thickly clustering trees. Beyond them came a pool of sunshine in which the old stone house basked like a huge grey cat itself. More garden was before it and beyond it, wonderful with blossom. Under a huge spreading beech tree in the centre of it was a little tea table; sitting by the table reading was a lady in a black dress.

The cat, having lured Jims to where he wanted him, sat down and began to lick his paws. He was quite willing to be caught now; but Jims had no longer any idea of catching him. He stood very still, looking at the lady. She did not see him then and Jims could only see her profile, which he thought very beautiful. She had wonderful ropes of blue-black hair wound around her head. She looked so sweet that Jims' heart beat. Then she lifted her head and turned her face and saw him. Jims felt something of a shock. She was not pretty after all. One side of her face was marked by a dreadful red scar. It quite spoilt her good looks, which Jims thought a great pity; but nothing could spoil the sweetness of her face or the loveliness of her peculiar soft, grey-blue eyes. Jims couldn't remember his mother and had no idea what she looked like, but the thought came into his head that he would have liked her to have eyes like that. After the first moment Jims did not mind the scar at all.

But perhaps that first moment had revealed itself in his face, for a look of pain came into the lady's eyes and, almost involuntarily it seemed, she put her hand up to hide the scar. Then she pulled it away again and sat looking at Jims half defiantly, half piteously. Jims thought she must be angry because he had chased her cat.

"I beg your pardon," he said gravely, "I didn't mean to hurt your cat. I just wanted to play with him. He is *such* a very handsome cat."

"But where did you come from?" said the lady. "It is so long since I saw a child in this garden," she added, as if to herself. Her voice was as sweet as her face. Jims thought he was mistaken in thinking her angry and plucked up heart of grace. Shyness was no fault of Jims.

"I came from the house over the wall," he said. "My name is James Brander Churchill. Aunt Augusta shut me up in the blue room because I spilled my pudding at dinner. I hate to be shut up. And I was to have had a ride this afternoon — and ice cream — and *maybe* a movie. So I was mad. And when your Very Handsome Cat came and looked at me I just got out and climbed down."

He looked straight at her and smiled. Jims had a very dear little smile. It seemed a pity there was no mother alive to revel in it. The lady smiled back.

"I think you did right," she said.

"*You* wouldn't shut a little boy up if you had one, would you?" said Jims.

"No — no, dear heart, I wouldn't," said the lady. She said it as if something hurt her horribly. She smiled again gallantly.

"Will you come here and sit down?" she added, pulling a chair out from the table.

"Thank you. I'd rather sit here," said Jims, plumping down on the grass at her feet. "Then maybe your cat will come to me."

The cat came over promptly and rubbed his head against Jims' knee. Jims stroked him delightedly; how lovely his soft fur felt and his round velvety head.

"I like cats," explained Jims, "and I have nothing but a gobbler. This is such a Very Handsome Cat. What is his name, please?"

"Black Prince. He loves me," said the lady. "He always comes to my bed in the morning and wakes me by patting my face with his paw. *He* doesn't mind my being ugly."

She spoke with a bitterness Jims couldn't understand.

"But you are not ugly," he said.

"Oh, I *am* ugly — I *am* ugly," she cried. "Just look at me — right at me. Doesn't it hurt you to look at me?"

Jims looked at her gravely and dispassionately.

"No, it doesn't," he said. "Not a bit," he added, after some further exploration of his consciousness.

Suddenly the lady laughed beautifully. A faint rosy flush came into her unscarred cheek.

"James, I believe you mean it."

"Of course I mean it. And, if you don't mind, please call me Jims. Nobody calls me James but Aunt Augusta. She isn't my whole aunt. She is just Uncle Walter's half-sister. *He* is my whole uncle."

"What does he call you?" asked the lady. She looked away as she asked it.

"Oh, Jims, when he thinks about me. He doesn't often think about me. He has too many sick children to think about. Sick children are all Uncle Walter cares about. He's the greatest children's doctor in the Dominion, Mr. Burroughs says. But he is a woman-hater."

"How do you know that?"

"Oh, I heard Mr. Burroughs say it. Mr. Burroughs is my tutor, you know. I study with him from nine till one. I'm not allowed to go to the public school. I'd like to, but Uncle Walter thinks I'm not strong enough yet. I'm going next year, though, when I'm ten. I have holidays now. Mr. Burroughs always goes away the first of June."

"How came he to tell you your uncle was a woman-hater?" persisted the lady.

"Oh, he didn't tell me. He was talking to a friend of his. He thought I was reading my book. So I was — but I heard it all. It was more interesting than my book. Uncle Walter was engaged to a lady, long, long ago, when he was a young man. She was devilishly pretty."

"Oh, Jims!"

"Mr. Burroughs said so. I'm only quoting," said Jims easily. "And Uncle Walter just worshipped her. And all at once she just jilted him without a word of explanation, Mr. Burroughs said. So that is why he hates women. It isn't any wonder, is it?"

"I suppose not," said the lady with a sigh. "Jims, are you hungry?"

"Yes, I am. You see, the pudding was spilled. But how did you know?"

"Oh, boys always used to be hungry when I knew them long ago. I thought they hadn't changed. I shall tell Martha to bring out something to eat and we'll have it here under this tree. You sit here — I'll sit there. Jims, it's so long since I talked to a little boy that I'm not sure that I know how."

"You know how, all right," Jims assured her. "But what am I to call you, please?"

"My name is Miss Garland," said the lady a little hesitatingly. But she saw the name meant nothing to Jims. "I would like you to call me Miss Avery. Avery is my first name and I never hear it nowadays. Now for a jamboree! I can't offer you a movie — and I'm afraid there isn't any ice cream either. I could have had some if I'd known you were coming. But I think Martha will be able to find something good."

A very old woman, who looked at Jims with great amazement, came out to set the table. Jims thought she must be as old as Methusaleh. But he did not mind her. He ran races with Black Prince while tea was being prepared, and rolled the delighted cat over and over in the grass. And he discovered a fragrant herb-garden in a far corner and was delighted. Now it was truly a garden of spices.

"Oh, it is so beautiful here," he told Miss Avery, who sat and looked at his revels with a hungry expression in her lovely eyes. "I wish I could come often."

"Why can't you?" said Miss Avery.

The two looked at each other with sly intelligence.

"I could come whenever Aunt Augusta shuts me up in the blue room," said Jims.

"Yes," said Miss Avery. Then she laughed and held out her arms. Jims flew into them. He put his arms about her neck and kissed her scarred face.

"Oh, I wish *you* were my aunt," he said.

Miss Avery suddenly pushed him away. Jims was horribly afraid he had offended her. But she took his hand.

"We'll just be chums, Jims," she said. "That's really better than being relations, after all. Come and have tea."

Over that glorious tea-table they became life-long friends. They had always known each other and always would. The Black Prince sat between them and was fed tit-bits. There was such a lot of good things on the table and nobody to say "You have had enough, James." James ate until *he* thought he had enough. Aunt Augusta would have thought he was doomed, could she have seen him.

"I suppose I must go back," said Jims with a sigh. "It will be our supper time in half an hour and Aunt Augusta will come to take me out."

"But you'll come again?"

"Yes, the first time she shuts me up. And if she doesn't shut me up pretty soon I'll be so bad she'll have to shut me up."

"I'll always set a place for you at the tea-table after this, Jims. And when you're not here I'll pretend you are. And when you can't come here write me a letter and bring it when you do come."

"Good-bye," said Jims. He took her hand and kissed it. He had read of a young knight doing that and had always thought he would like to try it if he ever got a chance. But who could dream of kissing Aunt Augusta's hands?

"You dear, funny thing," said Miss Avery. "Have you thought of how you are to get back? Can you reach that pine bough from the ground?"

"Maybe I can jump," said Jims dubiously.

"I'm afraid not. I'll give you a stool and you can stand on it. Just leave it there for future use. Good-bye, Jims. Jims, two hours ago I didn't know there was such a person in the world as you — and now I love you — I love you."

Jims' heart filled with a great warm gush of gladness. He had always wanted to be loved. And no living creature, he felt sure, loved him, except his gobbler — and a gobbler's love is not very satisfying, though it is better than nothing. He was blissfully happy as he carried his stool across the lawn. He climbed his pine and went in at the window and curled up on the seat in a maze of delight. The blue room was more shadowy than ever but that did not matter. Over in the Garden of Spices was friendship and laughter and romance galore. The whole world was transformed for Jims.

From that time Jims lived a shamelessly double life.

Whenever he was shut in the blue room he escaped to the Garden of Spices — and he was shut in very often, for, Mr. Burroughs being away, he got into a good deal of what Aunt Augusta called mischief. Besides, it is a sad truth that Jims didn't try very hard to be good now. He thought it paid better to be bad and be shut up. To be sure there was always a fly in the ointment. He was haunted by a vague fear that Aunt Augusta might relent and come to the blue room before supper time to let him out.

"And *then* the fat would be in the fire," said Jims.

But he had a glorious summer and throve so well on his new diet of love and companionship that one day Uncle Walter, with fewer sick children to think about than usual, looked at him curiously and said:

"Augusta, that boy seems to be growing much stronger. He has a good color and his eyes are getting to look more like a boy's eyes should. We'll make a man of you yet, Jims."

"He may be getting stronger but he's getting naughtier, too," said Aunt Augusta, grimly. "I am sorry to say, Walter, that he behaves very badly."

"We were all young once," said Uncle Walter indulgently.

"Were *you?*" asked Jims in blank amazement.

Uncle Walter laughed.

"Do you think me an antediluvian, Jims?"

"I don't know what *that* is. But your hair is gray and your eyes are tired," said Jims uncompromisingly.

Uncle Walter laughed again, tossed Jims a quarter, and went out.

"Your uncle is only forty-five and in his prime," said Aunt Augusta dourly.

Jims deliberately ran across the room to the window and, under pretence of looking out, knocked down a flower pot. So he was exiled to the blue room and got into his beloved Garden of Spices where Miss Avery's beautiful eyes looked love into his and the Black Prince was a jolly playmate and old Martha petted and spoiled him to her heart's content.

Jims never asked questions but he was a wide-awake chap, and, taking one thing with another, he found out a good deal about the occupants of the old stone house. Miss Avery never went anywhere and no one ever went there. She lived all alone with two old servants, man and maid. Except these two and Jims nobody had ever seen her for twenty years. Jims didn't know why, but he thought it must be because of the scar on her face.

He never referred to it, but one day Miss Avery told him what caused it.

"I dropped a lamp and my dress caught fire and burned my face, Jims. It made me hideous. I was beautiful before that — very beautiful. Everybody said so. Come in and I will show you my picture."

She took him into her big parlor and showed him the picture hanging on the wall between the two high windows. It was of a young girl in white. She certainly was very lovely, with her rose-leaf skin and laughing eyes. Jims looked at the pictured face gravely, with his hands in his pockets and his head on one side. Then he looked at Miss Avery.

"You were prettier then — yes," he said, judicially, "but I like your face ever so much better now."

"Oh, Jims, you can't," she protested.

"Yes, I do," persisted Jims. "You look kinder and— nicer now."

It was the nearest Jims could get to expressing what he felt as he looked at the picture. The young girl was beautiful, but her face was a little hard. There was pride and vanity and something of the insolence of great beauty in it. There was nothing of that in Miss Avery's face now — nothing but sweetness and tenderness, and a motherly yearning to which every fibre of Jims' small being responded. How they loved each other, those two! And how they understood each other! To *love* is easy, and therefore common; but to *understand* — how rare that is! And oh! such good times as they had! They made taffy. Jims had always longed to make taffy, but Aunt Augusta's immaculate kitchen and saucepans might not be so desecrated. They read fairy tales together. Mr. Burroughs had disapproved of fairy tales. They blew soap-bubbles out on the lawn and let them float away over the garden and the orchard like fairy balloons. They had glorious afternoon teas under the beech tree. They made ice cream themselves. Jims even slid down the bannisters when he wanted to. And he could try out a slang word or two occasionally without anybody dying of horror. Miss Avery did not seem to mind it a bit.

At first Miss Avery always wore dark sombre dresses. But one day Jims found her in a pretty gown of pale primrose silk. It was very old and old-fashioned, but Jims did not know that. He capered round her in delight.

"You like me better in this?" she asked, wistfully.

"I like you just as well, no matter what you wear," said Jims, "but that dress is awfully pretty."

"Would you like me to wear bright colors, Jims?"

"You bet I would," said Jims emphatically.

After that she always wore them — pink and primrose and blue and white; and she let Jims wreathe flowers in her splendid hair. He had quite a knack of it. She never wore any jewelry except, always, a little gold ring with a design of two clasped hands.

"A friend gave that to me long ago when we were boy and girl together at school," she told Jims once. "I never take it off, night or day. When I die it is to be buried with me."

"You mustn't die till I do," said Jims in dismay.

"Oh, Jims, if we could only *live* together nothing else would matter," she said hungrily. "Jims—Jims—I see so little of you really — and some day soon you'll be going to school — and I'll lose you."

"I've got to think of some way to prevent it," cried Jims.

"I won't have it. I won't — I won't."

But his heart sank notwithstanding.

One day Jims slipped from the blue room, down the pine and across the lawn with a tear-stained face.

"Aunt Augusta is going to kill my gobbler," he sobbed in Miss Avery's arms. "She says she isn't going to bother with him any longer — and he's getting old — and he's to be killed. And that gobbler is the only friend I have in the world except you. Oh, I can't *stand* it, Miss Avery."

Next day Aunt Augusta told him the gobbler had been sold and taken away. And Jims flew into a passion of tears and protest about it and was promptly incarcerated in the blue room. A few minutes later a sobbing boy plunged through the trees — and stopped abruptly. Miss Avery was reading under the beech and the Black Prince was snoozing on her knee — and a big, magnificent, bronze turkey was parading about on the lawn, twisting his huge fan of a tail this way and that.

"*My* gobbler!" cried Jims.

"Yes. Martha went to your uncle's house and bought him. Oh, she didn't betray you. She told Nancy Jane she wanted a gobbler and, having seen one over there, thought perhaps she could get him. See, here's your pet, Jims, and here he shall live till he dies of old age. And I have something else for you — Edward and Martha went across the river yesterday to the Murray Kennels and got it for you."

"Not a dog?" exclaimed Jims.

"Yes — a dear little bull pup. He shall be your very own, Jims, and I only stipulate that you reconcile the Black Prince to him."

It was something of a task but Jims succeeded. Then followed a month of perfect happiness. At least three afternoons a week they contrived to be together. It was all too good to be true, Jims felt. Something would happen soon to spoil it. Just *suppose* Aunt Augusta grew tender-hearted and ceased to punish! Or suppose she suddenly discovered that he was growing too big to be shut up! Jims began to stint himself in eating lest he grew too fast. And then Aunt Augusta worried about his loss of appetite and suggested to Uncle Walter that he should be sent to the country till the hot weather was over. Jims didn't want to go to the country now because his heart was elsewhere. He must eat again, if he grew like a weed. It was all very harassing.

Uncle Walter looked at him keenly.

"It seems to me you're looking pretty fit, Jims. Do you want to go to the country?"

"No, please."

"Are you happy, Jims?"

"Sometimes."

"A boy should be happy all the time, Jims."

"If I had a mother and someone to play with I would be."

"I have tried to be a mother to you, Jims," said Aunt Augusta, in an offended tone. Then she addressed Uncle Walter. "A younger woman would probably understand him better. And I feel that the care of this big place is too much for me. I would prefer to go to my own old home. If you had married long ago, as you should, Walter, James would have had a mother and some cousins to play with. I have always been of this opinion."

Uncle Walter frowned and got up.

"Just because one woman played you false is no good reason for spoiling your life," went on Aunt Augusta severely. "I have kept silence all these years but now I am going to speak — and speak plainly. You should marry, Walter. You are young enough yet and you owe it to your name."

"Listen, Augusta," said Uncle Walter sternly. "I loved a woman once. I believed she loved me. She sent me back my ring one day and with it a message saying she had ceased to care for me and bidding me never to try to look upon her face again. Well, I have obeyed her, that is all."

"There was something strange about all that, Walter.

The life she has since led proves that. So you should not let it embitter you against all women."

"I haven't. It's nonsense to say I'm a woman-hater, Augusta. But that experience has robbed me of the power to care for another woman."

"Well, this isn't a proper conversation for a child to hear," said Aunt Augusta, recollecting herself. "Jims, go out."

Jims would have given one of his ears to stay and listen with the other. But he went obediently.

And then, the very next day, the dreaded something happened.

It was the first of August and very, very hot. Jims was late coming to dinner and Aunt Augusta reproved him and Jims, deliberately, and with malice aforethought, told her he thought she was a nasty old woman. He had never been saucy to Aunt Augusta before. But it was three days since he had seen Miss Avery and the Black Prince and Nip and he was desperate. Aunt Augusta crimsoned with anger and doomed Jims to an afternoon in the blue room for impertinence.

"And I shall tell your uncle when he comes home," she added.

That rankled, for Jims didn't want Uncle Walter to think him impertinent. But he forgot all his worries as he scampered through the Garden of Spices to the beech tree. And there Jims stopped as if he had been shot. Prone on the grass under the beech tree, white and cold and still, lay his Miss Avery — dead, stone dead!

At least Jims thought she was dead. He flew into the house like a mad thing, shrieking for Martha. Nobody answered. Jims recollected, with a rush of sickening dread, that Miss Avery had told him Martha and Edward were going away that day to visit a sister. He rushed blindly across the lawn again, through the little side gate he had never passed before and down the street home. Uncle Walter was just opening the door of his car.

156

"Uncle Walter — come — come," sobbed Jims, clutching frantically at his hand. 'Miss Avery's dead — dead — oh, come quick."

"*Who* is dead?"

"Miss Avery — Miss Avery Garland. She's lying on the grass over there in her garden. And I love her so — and I'll die, too — oh, Uncle Walter, *come.*"

Uncle Walter looked as if he wanted to ask some questions, but he said nothing. With a strange face he hurried after Jims. Miss Avery was still lying there. As Uncle Walter bent over her he saw the broad red scar and started back with an exclamation.

"She is dead?" gasped Jims.

"No," said Uncle Walter, bending down again — "no, she has only fainted, Jims — overcome by the heat, I suppose. I want help. Go and call somebody."

"There's no one home here to-day," said Jims, in a spasm of joy so great that it shook him like a leaf.

"Then go home and telephone over to Mr. Loring's. Tell them I want the nurse who is there to come here for a few minutes."

Jims did his errand. Uncle Walter and the nurse carried Miss Avery into the house and then Jims went back to the blue room. He was so unhappy he didn't care where he went. He wished something *would* jump at him out of the bed and put an end to him. Everything was discovered now and he would never see Miss Avery again. Jims lay very still on the window seat. He did not even cry. He had come to one of the griefs that lie too deep for tears.

"I think I must have been put under a curse at birth," thought poor Jims.

* * *

Over at the stone house Miss Avery was lying on the couch in her room. The nurse had gone away and Dr. Walter was sitting looking at her. He leaned forward and pulled away the hand with which she was hiding the scar on her face. He looked first at the little gold ring on the hand and then at the scar.

"Don't," she said piteously.

"Avery — why did you do it? — *why* did you do it?"

"Oh, you know — you must know now, Walter."

"Avery, did you break my heart and spoil my life — and your own — simply because your face was scarred?"

"I couldn't bear to have you see me hideous," she moaned. "You had been so proud of my beauty. I — I — thought you couldn't love me any more — I couldn't bear the thought of looking in your eyes and seeing aversion there."

Walter Grant leaned forward.

"Look in my eyes, Avery. Do you see any aversion?"

Avery forced herself to look. What she saw covered her face with a hot blush.

"Did you think my love such a poor and superficial thing, Avery," he said sternly, "that it must vanish because a blemish came on your fairness? Do you think *that* would change me? Was your own love for me so slight?"

"No — no," she sobbed. "I have loved you every moment of my life, Walter. Oh, don't look at me so sternly."

"If you had even told me," he said. "You said I was never to try to look on your face again — and they told me you had gone away. You sent me back my ring."

"I kept the old one," she interrupted, holding out her hand, "the first one you ever gave me — do you remember, Walter? When we were boy and girl."

"You robbed me of all that made life worth while, Avery. Do you wonder that I've been a bitter man?"

"I was wrong — I was wrong," she sobbed. "I should have believed in you. But don't you think I've paid, too? Forgive me, Walter — it's too late to atone — but forgive me."

"*Is* it too late?" he asked gravely.

She pointed to the scar.

"Could you endure seeing this opposite to you every day at your table?" she asked bitterly.

"Yes — if I could see your sweet eyes and your beloved smile with it, Avery," he answered passionately. "Oh, Avery, it was *you* I loved — not your outward favor. Oh, how foolish you were — foolish and morbid! You always put too high a value on beauty, Avery. If I had dreamed of the true state of the case — if I had known you were here all these years — why I heard a rumor long ago that you had married, Avery — but if I had known I would have come to you and *made* you be — sensible."

She gave a little laugh at his lame conclusion. That was so like the old Walter. Then her eyes filled with tears as he took her in his arms.

* * *

The door of the blue room opened. Jims did not look up. It was Aunt Augusta, of course — and she had heard the whole story.

"Jims, boy."

Jims lifted his miserable eyes. It was Uncle Walter — but a different Uncle Walter — an Uncle Walter with laughing eyes and a strange radiance of youth about him.

"Poor, lonely little fellow," said Uncle Walter unexpectedly. "Jims, would you like Miss Avery to come *here* — and live with us always — and be your real aunt?"

"Great snakes!" said Jims, transformed in a second. "Is there any chance of *that*?"

"There is a certainty, thanks to you," said Uncle Walter. "You can go over to see her for a little while. Don't talk her to death — she's weak yet — and attend to that menagerie of yours over there — she's worrying because the bull dog and gobbler weren't fed — and, Jims —"

But Jims had swung down through the pine and was tearing across the Garden of Spices.

The Bride Is Waiting

Since it was Saturday Susan did not have to go to the college so there was little to divert her mind from the disturbing thought that it was her thirtieth birthday.

Aunt Ada had apparently forgotten it . . . although she had mentioned casually at the breakfast table that she noticed several gray hairs in Susan's sleek, dark head. Aunt Ada would mention things like that. Susan knew the gray hairs were there. It did not matter, she had told herself when she had first discovered them. Nothing like that had mattered since the telegram had come so many years ago bearing the brief, terrible tidings of Vernon Darby's death at Vimy Ridge. It did not matter if all her hair turned gray . . . like her life. Gray and lustreless. But was that any reason why everyone should forget her birthday?

Even Ellery had forgotten it. It was the first birthday for ten years that he had not sent her roses. But more likely he had not forgotten . . . probably he was just being odiously tactful. He might have thought that a girl would not care to have it said, even with roses, that she was thirty. She wasn't going to think about such things at all. Nobody cared whether the teacher of Modern Languages at Clement's were thirty or fifty so long as she was efficient.

But even that reflection did not help her to forget that she was thirty. That fact kept bobbing up at every breathing spell. Thirty *did* sound so horribly much older than twenty-nine. And yet there was still so much of life ahead to be lived through somehow. Lived through as a drab teacher of Modern Languages to girls whose only use for any language, ancient or modern, seemed to be talking to and about boys. Susan was not often as unjust to the girls as that. But, she reflected darkly, the arrival of thirty did things to you.

She had been very conscious of its approach for some weeks. And she had been wondering if, after all, it would not be wiser to tell Ellery she would marry him when her birthday came and brought with it his annual proposal. Ellery had such a confirmed habit of asking her to marry him on her birthdays. She never seemed able to convince him that she meant to be forever faithful to the memory of Vernon Darby. And now . . . well, she would be faithful, in a way, as somebody had said. It couldn't really be considered unfaithful to make the best of what remained for herself and Ellery. They had always been good pals ever since their High School days. She could never, she believed, give him the love that was buried somewhere in France but real companionship meant much. She had decided that she would tell him graciously that if he were satisfied with what she could give him she would marry him. She felt that she was being very kind to Ellery in this decision and that he ought to be very appreciative and grateful. Susan found herself looking forward to his happiness. It would be wonderful to make him happy, even if she could be nothing more than merely contented herself. It was, of course, impossible for her ever to love anybody again. But there were substitutes.

When Ellery Boyden dropped in rather late that evening he did not bring any roses. Susan had seen him coming up the street, with Banjo loping at his heels. Evidently she was to be the fag-end of his evening's hike. She sighed a little . . . she breathed a prayer to Vernon for pardon . . . she went forward to accept her destiny and Ellery.

An hour later Susan was feeling decidedly let down. Ellery did not seem to have the slightest intention of proposing. He lounged deliberately in the chair he affected and talked of a score of things that ought to have been interesting. Banjo, a gay little dog with a hint of wistfulness behind his gayety, lay on the floor at Susan's feet with his head on her shoe. Susan loved Banjo but as the time wore on she had a perverse inclination to pull her foot away and let Banjo look elsewhere for a pillow.

Ellery had suddenly fallen silent. Susan perked up a bit. Perhaps it was coming after all.

The first signs were about as usual. Ellery cleared his throat, uncrossed his legs and crossed them again. So far, normal. But Ellery was nervous. Susan had never before seen Ellery nervous on the occasion of his annual proposal. Did he, too, feel that things had drifted long enough and that it was time for a definite decision?

"I've really come to ask a favour of you, Susan," said Ellery jerkily. "A great . . . favour."

This was a new gambit. Susan pricked up her ears. But she did not pull away her foot from Banjo's head. He was such a darling dog.

"I'm sure there's nobody in the world for whom I'd sooner do a favour," she said graciously. If it is in my power, that is."

"Oh, it's in your power all right," said Ellery. "In fact you are the very one. You have such perfect taste."

Was the man going to ask her to pick out a neck-tie? He couldn't be proposing. Susan did not wholly pull her foot away but she jerked it and Banjo moaned a protest in his sleep.

"I . . . I've bought a house," said Ellery. He seemed to have difficulty in speaking. Something was embarassing him horribly. "And I want . . . that is . . . I'd like . . . would you mind very much . . . helping me to furnish it?"

So it *was* a proposal after all. Susan smiled to herself in the twilight. It was to be baited with a house this time. Fancy Ellery buying a house, the poor darling! As if she would marry him for a house! How clever he thought himself! And how unnecessary it all was when she had already made up her mind to marry him for other and better reasons.

"Why," she said slowly, "I'm afraid I don't know very much about furnishing a house, Ellery."

"Oh, you know all about such things," said Ellery positively. "I'd make a frightful botch of it, I know. I'd mix Victorian and Georgian and Modernistic all up together and the result would be a nightmare. You can picture it for yourself."

Susan could. But she was not going to surrender too easily . . . and certainly not to a house. Ellery must be shown that his new dodge was unfortunate.

"But you see, Ellery, my taste mightn't suit the . . . the mistress of the house."

"Oh, it would . . . I'm sure it would." Ellery was more eager than ever. "I know Juanita will love anything you select."

Juanita! Susan pulled away her foot and Banjo woke up. He looked at her reproachfully and then went over and sat down beside Ellery. His expression said plainly:

"I am fond of you, Susan . . . but if there's to be a difference of opinion between you and Ellery you might as well know at once where I stand."

"Who is Juanita?" Susan heard herself asking.

"The girl I'm going to marry," said Ellery explosively. "Juanita Vaughan. I met her last Christmas when I was down home. She's . . . she's an angel, Susan."

"I suppose so." Susan had had enough time to recover from . . . well, from her surprise. What else? Anybody would be surprised by such an unexpected piece of news. Susan laughed a little. She did not laugh often but when she did her laughter was generally beautiful. It did not sound exactly beautiful just now but Ellery was in no condition of mind to notice that. "This *is* a real birthday surprise, Ellery."

"Oh, . . . to be sure . . . this *is* your birthday," said

Ellery confusedly. "I'd forgotten . . . I was buying the house . . . I'm sorry."

"Don't be," said Susan graciously. "You couldn't be expected to remember birthdays under the circumstances. Besides . . . when one is thirty one prefers such forgetfulness. As for this news of yours, Ellery . . . now that I've got my breath . . . I'm so very glad to hear it. As an old friend there's no happiness I don't wish you. But you might have told me before, I think . . . I really do."

"There wasn't anything to tell . . . till just a few days ago. I mean . . . it wasn't settled. You are the first one I've told. I . . . I knew you'd be glad I wasn't going to keep on being foolish forever. We'll always be good pals, Susan, won't we?"

"Naturally. I couldn't see us being anything else," said Susan more graciously still.

"And Juanita . . . you'll be her friend too, won't you? She'll need a good friend . . . she's so young . . . a mere baby. . . ."

"I can't imagine your wife and I *not* being friends, Ellery."

"I knew you'd see it like that," said Ellery triumphantly. "You're such a darling, dependable old sport, Susan. And about the house . . . you'll help me, won't you."

"I'll see what I can do, if you think my point of view will suit . . . Juanita. What house have you bought?"

"Dan Weaver's house up on the hill . . . Cat's Ladder . . . you know it."

Yes, Susan knew it. She and Ellery had passed it on one of their hikes and she had exclaimed enthusiastically over it. Susan loved nice houses. All her life she had lived in Aunt Ada's big, handsome, hideous one, in its bare treeless lot, and hated it. But the Weaver place . . . Cat's Ladder, Dan had named it because of the steep ravine behind it . . . had beckoned to her as an unquestioned member of its tribe. And now she was to furnish it for Juanita. "I rushed off to buy it as soon as Juanita wrote me that she

164

would marry me," said Ellery. "I . . . it *belonged* to her . . . I could see her in it. She's . . . she's beautiful, Susan."

"I'm sure you wouldn't choose anyone who wasn't," said Susan, more gracious every time she spoke. It did not occur to either her or Ellery that she was really paying herself quite a handsome compliment. "What is she like . . . I mean, what is her type? I'll have to know something about that if I'm to furnish her house for her. But really, Ellery, wouldn't it be better to wait till you're married and let her do her own furnishing? I'm sure *I* wouldn't like another woman to furnish my house for me."

"No . . . but Juanita's different," said Ellery out of a dreamy rapture. "She's only a child . . . and she's always had everything done for her . . . one of the Edgetown Vaughans, you know. She isn't a bit efficient, Susan. . . ." Susan flinched . . . "And I don't want her bothered about practical things. I've set my heart on getting my home all ready for her . . . and bringing her there."

"Carrying her in over the threshold, I suppose," said Susan a trifle sarcastically.

"Yes, just that," said Ellery simply. "It will be easy . . . she's so . . . so girlish. As for her type, Juanita should be dark of course, with a name like that . . . but she is as fair as the moon. With sparkling hair and soft, radiant, dark-green eyes. . . . I never knew how beautiful green eyes could be until I saw Juanita . . . a shy, ethereal creature with a Madonna face."

"And I'm to furnish Cat's Ladder to suit *that*," said Susan in a tone of mock dismay. "When . . . when is the wedding to be?"

"In late August, I hope. That will give us time for a month in Muskoka."

"And this is mid-May. Three months. Well, I'll do my best, Ellery."

"Thank you." Ellery got up with an air of relief. "You've taken a weight off what's left of my mind, Susan. Come, Banjo."

Banjo went. But at the door he turned and looked back at Susan. "I have to stand by *him* you understand . . . but not by *her*," he said plainly.

Susan, after a few minutes alone in the spring night, ran singing upstairs. Aunt Ada looked out from her room.

"What is the matter, child?"

"Matter? Why, nothing is the matter," said Susan. "I'm singing."

"You never sing except when something is bothering you."

"Nothing is bothering me," said Susan decidedly. "Nothing at all. I'm delighted and excited. I've a summer of pure delight ahead of me . . . I've promised to furnish a home for Ellery Boyden and his bride . . . one of the Edgetown Vaughans, you know. Who wouldn't sing over such a prospect?"

"Well," said Aunt Ada consolingly, "there are as good fish in the sea as ever come out of it."

Susan shut her door with a bang. No use arguing with Aunt Ada. Aunt Ada would never believe that her heart was buried in France. Susan had suddenly gone back to this belief herself. She went and looked at herself in the mirror. Well, she was not in the least like Juanita Vaughan. She, Susan, was tall and black-haired . . . black *yet* . . . with brook-brown eyes. She certainly couldn't be conveniently carried over anybody's threshold. But wasn't her air of distinction getting a little shop worn?

"Ellery is thirty-five and he is marrying a baby," she said contemptuously. "Evidently being Professor of Economics and Sociology in Clement college doesn't make a man sensible when it comes to choosing a wife. Well, laugh at yourself, Susan, dear. This is the very time for your noted sense of humour to function. Sitting, all dressed up on your thirtieth birthday, confidently expecting to be proposed to. And the man in the case comes and asks you to . . . furnish a house for his fair, ethereal bride. Why, it's a picture for the comic strip, Susan."

"I've seen a good many houses I liked," said Ellery. "They would *do*. But when I saw this house I knew I had to have it. You remember that evening a year ago, when we were out for mayflowers, Susan, and took this short cut home? We both looked up and saw it at the same time."

"*Recognized* it although we'd never seen it before," said Susan dreamily. "I've always want . . . loved a white and green house."

Cat's Ladder was even more charming than she remembered it. Houses with charm always thrilled Susan . . . they were so rare. What a view! The city spread far below them . . . the college campus to the left . . . the beautiful tower of the memorial library framed between two slender lombardies against a soft, flushed evening sky . . . dreamy hills to the right, with an exquisite valley between.

"Some valleys are so lovable," Ellery was saying. "Just to look at them gives you pleasure. That valley is one of them. But that tree must come down, mustn't it?"

"That lovely maple . . . oh, you'd never cut *that* down," cried Susan, who loved trees with passion.

"It spoils the view," defended Ellery.

"It doesn't . . . it simply guards it as a treasure. And can't you see what dignity and beauty and romance it lends to that corner. I am sure Juanita will love that tree."

Susan wasn't any too sure of it really. She felt that green-eyed creatures never could love trees. But Ellery had no misgivings.

"Yes, she will. So we'll leave it. When I come to think of it, it will be just the place to have breakfast under on summer mornings. We'll have breakfast out-of-doors whenever possible. Look at that far hill over there, Susan. It is a friend of mine. Doesn't it seem like a remote, austere old man in this light? But in other lights it grows mellow and lovable. We'll have a garden in that sunny corner. I must have larkspur and columbine . . . foxgloves and white iris . . . and Canterbury bells, white, pink, delicious mauve flecked with purple. The gardens in Edgetown are full of them."

"Will your lady of the sparkling hair like such old-fashioned flowers?" asked Susan spitefully.

"She loves everything beautiful," said Ellery fatuously.

Susan couldn't endure fatuousness so she went inside to have a look over the interior. She hoped to be able to find lots of faults . . . things that would make it easy to let Mrs. Ellery Boyden have the house. But she couldn't find one. The sunny dining-room with its recessed window, shaded with wistaria, was Susan's idea of a dining-room. There was lovely shadow tapestry on the walls when the sunlight fell through the leaves. The living-room, with the two pointed firs before its east window, really lived. The quaint window on the stair landing with the broad, deep seat where one could sit and look down into the ravine was not a window . . . it was a personality.

"Don't you think she'll love the view from this window?" asked Ellery. "I'm glad all my windows have a beautiful view. There is some special loveliness to be seen from each one of them. I want her dear eyes to see nothing but beauty whenever she looks out of my house."

Susan reflected that falling in love did have a tendency to make people sentimental. But she was very tolerant. And Cat's Ladder had such possibilities. She found herself taking a keen interest in them. To her surprise the following weeks were full of interest. Susan put out of her mind all thought of Juanita and decided she would furnish Cat's Ladder to suit her own taste.

"There's no use trying to do anything else. I don't know Juanita in spite of Ellery's raptures and it is of no use doing up the house according to my hazy conception of her. Ellery must trust me all in all or not at all when it comes to a question of tastes."

Ellery was very trusting. Beyond telling Susan she need not worry over prices he interfered very little. She dragged him about a good bit hunting for things that belonged to

Cat's Ladder and they had some arguments but Ellery always gave in. Susan had a nose for quaint findings and the delightful old brass knocker she found in a dilapidated Jew's shop on the east side made her weep with joy. Ellery's old Persian rug, with the tree of life woven in it, went on the living room floor, although Ellery wanted to buy something new and bright. There was a beautiful old grandfather clock and an oak settee for the hall. Susan picked up lovely old pictures with printed legends on them and charming old blue platters and hand-wrought iron candlesticks. There was a Stuart table with twist-turned legs that Ellery's grandmother had had and Susan insisted on putting his sea-captain uncle's mahogany chest of drawers in the living-room, although Ellery thought it should be smuggled out of sight in some back bedroom.

"It's the loveliest thing you have," said Susan severely.

They spent a wholly delightful afternoon looking over everything in it. Ellery had never troubled to go through it before. He was amazed. Corals . . . pink and white and potted shells . . . feathers of strange tropical birds . . . seeds and nuts from mid-sea islands . . . ivory idols . . . wonderful embroideries.

"Isn't it delightful unpacking these old drawers? You don't know what we may come across," said Susan happily. "Oh!" she pounced on something in a tiny box with a squeal of delight. "What is it? Oh, Ellery, it's a little real pearl . . . an unpolished pearl! Isn't it a darling thing?"

"I must have that set in a ring for Juanita," said Ellery.

Susan had forgotten Juanita in the wonders of that chest. She got up, a little pale and cross. She was tired. She had spent all the forenoon in a department store, since an Edgetown Vaughan's home could not be wholly furnished with antiques. At that, it was fascinating to go into a big store and pick things to buy . . . pretty things that just wanted to take away from all the glitter and too-muchness to be made part of a real home. She had spent several sleepless nights over Ellery's window draperies but the result justified her loss of slumber. Though Susan found she was having too many sleepless nights, even when there was no question of window draperies. It was a hot summer and furniture hunting was strenuous work. Her nerves were going. Things were beginning to annoy her. That light in Ellery's eyes whenever he talked of Juanita, for example. And that little gold cushion on the window seat. Ellery had bought that off his own bat. He told her that he wanted it because he could picture Juanita's paler gold of hair against its warm background. Susan hated it. And she thought it very silly. It would make golden hair look pale and faded.

"Juanita should have a lovely dull green. That cushion belongs to dark ladies."

"I'm sure it will suit her," said Ellery stubbornly. "I love to picture that thistledown charm of hers in this dim corner against this gold cushion. She'll look like a Madonna with an aureole."

So the cushion continued to glow like a small sun on the dark window-seat and Susan's fingers tingled to hurl it down the ravine every time she saw it. Thistledown charm, forsooth!

Everything else she loved. And there was so much to love now. It was late July and Cat's Ladder was complete in every detail. Susan went over it and its perfection tore anew at her heart. That it should be wasted on a child whose only conception of a house was a place to eat and sleep in, during the intervals of making whoopee. She had gathered from Ellery that Juanita was fond of a good time. Ellery really talked too much about Juanita. Under the circumstances a little reserve would be in better taste. But Susan listened patiently and pretended to be sympathetic and understanding. And under everything was a sense of deep satisfaction in something well done. So well done that it would be hard for even Juanita to spoil it or undo it. Susan thought of a house she had been in that day . . . the chair coverings too vivid . . . the pictures arranged horribly

. . . the lampshades unforgivable . . . the lighting all wrong
. . . the rugs all wrong . . . the angles of the furniture all
wrong. Susan shuddered and thanked Heaven for the con-
trast of Cat's Ladder.

"Cat's Ladder is ready for your bride," she told Ellery
one hot July evening. She was lying listlessly on her chair;
she had been too tired to do up her shabby face and she
looked pale and . . . *old,* she told herself fiercely.

"How can I ever thank you?" said Ellery humbly.

"Don't bother," said Susan listlessly. "Why should you?
I've had my fun out of it. I've really enjoyed doing up that
place. When is the wedding to be, Ellery?"

"It's not quite settled yet. I'm expecting to know the
final date any day now. I . . . I hope it will be soon. Susan,
you look tired."

"Dragged to death, as Aunt Ada informed me at supper
time. Aunt Ada is so comforting. You must remember I'm
over thirty, Ellery. People begin to get tired when youth is
past. Banjo, why are you sitting there on your tail, grinning at me? Ellery, will Juanita like Banjo? Will she let
him bring his bones into the house?"

"I'm afraid Juanita doesn't care much for dogs. She
seems a little afraid of them. I must get her a cat. She is
fond of cats."

"How will Banjo get on with a cat?"

"He'll have to get used to it."

"They say one can get used to everything even to being
hanged," sighed Susan. "I've never believed it. Poor little
dorglums! Even a dog ought to have some rights, oughtn't
he, Ellery? Do you think you are going to be quite fair
to Banjo?"

"There she is singing again," thought Aunt Ada, as
Susan went to her room. "Susan has never sung so much as
she has this summer. I do hope she will soon be in better
spirits."

*   *   *

Ellery telephoned up at five o'clock one fine blue evening

and asked Susan if she would meet him at Cat's Ladder around eight. He had something to tell her. She knew what it was . . . the date of his wedding day. Well, she wasn't interested. When you are horribly tired you can't care about anything. You cannot love or hate or weep or jest. But she made up her mind she would go up to Cat's Ladder at seven and have one last hour of it before Ellery came. And say good-bye to it.

Cat's Ladder had never looked so beautiful . . . so *happy*. Susan had never felt so close to it . . . so *one* with it. She loved it as much as she hated Juanita. For she did hate Juanita . . . she admitted that to herself at last. It was torture to think of Juanita being mistress of Cat's Ladder . . . moving the furniture about . . . sitting by the fireplace . . . laughing at Banjo when everyone knew he couldn't bear to be laughed at . . . handling the dishes . . . Susan clenched her hands. She couldn't bear the thought of Juanita handling the dishes. Suppose she, Susan, simply smashed them all now. Especially that darling robin's-egg pitcher with the little golden roses on it. Juanita shouldn't have that . . . Susan couldn't bear it . . . she would smash *it* anyhow. She ran to the mantel-piece and seized it. Then she saw herself in the mirror . . . and set the pitcher back. Heavens, what a thin, withered, efficient old woman she was going to make! All alone . . . with no interest in life! She hated Juanita . . . beautiful Juanita who had never made her green eyes dim poring over exam papers. Just at that moment Susan could cheerfully have handed her a poisoned philtre of Borgia brewing.

"Come out and see the sunset," said Ellery by the door.

"I've seen hundreds of sunsets. Is there anything special about this one?" asked Susan grumpily. She had no intention of going out. Here in the twilight she need not smile bravely. Susan felt that her face would simply crack in two if she smiled just once again when Ellery mentioned Juanita.

"There is always something special about any sunset,"

said Ellery. But he came in and sat down beside her on the divan. He did not say anything at first. And Susan wouldn't speak . . . *couldn't* speak. She was horrified to find herself trembling . . . to find herself a boiling, seething volcano of hate and rage and fury and despair . . . she who had been so certain that she could never feel deeply about anything again. She hated Juanita more savagely than ever . . . Juanita who was to have *her* house and her man . . . yes, her man! Vernon Darby had suddenly become nothing save a pale phantom of Vimy Ridge.

"Just think, Susan," Ellery said at last, "in two more months my lady will be here . . . my little queen. It seems . . ." his voice dropped reverently ". . . too wonderful to be true. Susan, do you think that by any chance I'm only dreaming?"

Perhaps if Ellery had never given tongue to that terrible bromide, "little queen", Susan might not have quite lost her self-control. But it was the last straw. She stood up.

"Yes, I think you are, you abysmal idiot," she said furiously. "You *are* an idiot to think of marrying a young girl . . . a brainless, empty, beautiful little fool without two ideas in her skull, as pretty and insipid as a movie star. Dreaming . . . yes. And you'll waken up with a vengeance when it's too late . . . and nobody will pity you . . . everybody will laugh at you . . ."

Susan choked on a hysterical peal of laughter. Ellery stood up.

"Ah, now, that's something like," he said in a tone of satisfaction. "I think if you had kept up your smiling, indifferent pose of sympathetic pal and comrade one minute longer I would have brained you with that brass and iron. You don't know what narrow risks of assassination you've run this summer. As for Juanita, I agree with you that she is too young for me . . . much. I've felt that all along. But don't call her brainless and empty. She is amazingly intelligent . . . for a child who was five her last birthday. She's really a darling, Susan . . . I'm sure you'll love her when we go to Edgetown for Christmas."

Susan stopped laughing and looked at Ellery. Ellery looked back with a sheepish grin.

"Gad, how I hate to explain! Still, it's bliss to have the luxury of telling the truth again after my orgy of lies. But I *did* tell you that Juanita was a mere baby, didn't I? So much was profoundly true. And I had to do something, Susan, to show you that . . . that . . ."

"That what I thought was devotion was only a sentimental thrall of yesterday," said Susan slowly. She felt that she ought to be angry . . . but she could only feel shamelessly glad.

"No, but that you really did care for me if you would only let yourself see it. Remember, I had to fight a ghost. I was desperate . . . I realized that it was my last chance. What say, Susan? Cat's Ladder is ready for its mistress and only you can be that?"

"I ought to hate you . . . and throw Cat's Ladder in your face . . . and leave you," said Susan. "But I can't . . . I just can't. Instead, I . . . I . . . think I'm going to cry on your shoulder."

# I Know
A Secret

"I know a secret . . . I know a secret . . . I know a secret . . . and I won't tell *you*," chanted Dovie Johnson as she teetered back and forth on the very edge of the wharf.

Jane shuddered to see her, and yet the teetering had a fascination. She was so sure Dovie would fall off sometime, and then what? But Dovie never did. Her luck always held.

Everything Dovie did, or said she did — which were, perhaps, two very different things, although Jane was too innocent and credulous to know that — had a fascination for Jane. Dovie, who was eleven and had lived in Bartibog all her life, knew so much more than Jane, who was only eight and had lived in Bartibog only a year. Bartibog, Dovie said, was the only place where people knew anything. What could you know, shut up in a town?

And Dovie knew so many secrets. She never would tell them, and Jane pined to know them. Secrets must be such wonderful, mysterious, beautiful things. Jane hadn't a single secret. Everything she knew, other people knew — Mother and Aunt Helen and Uncle George. And a secret wasn't a secret if more than two people knew it, so Dovie said. If Dovie would only tell her one single secret, that would be enough. But plead as Jane might and did, Dovie wouldn't. Dovie would only wrinkle up her fat nose and look important and say that Jane was far too young to have secrets. This maddened Jane.

"You'd tell somebody. You couldn't help it," taunted Dovie.

"I wouldn't — I could so," cried Jane. "Oh, Dovie,

please tell me a secret, just one. You know so many. You might tell me just one. Dovie—" Jane had a sudden inspiration — "if you tell me a secret, I'll give you six apples for it."

Dovie's queer little amber eyes gleamed. Apples were apples in Bartibog, where orchards were few. The George Lawrences had a small one, and in it were some August apples that ripened sooner than any others in Bartibog.

"Six yellow apples off that tree in the southwest corner?" bargained Dovie.

Jane nodded. Her breath came quickly. Was it—oh, was it possible that Dovie would really tell her a secret?

"Will your aunt let you?" demanded Dovie.

Every one in Bartibog knew that Mrs. George Lawrence was as mean as second skimmings with her apples, as with everything else. Jane nodded again, but rather uncertainly. She was none too sure about it. Aunt Helen let her have one apple a day — "to keep the doctor away" — but six all at once were a pretty big order. Dovie scented the uncertainty.

"You would have to have those apples right here before I could tell you a secret," she said firmly. "No apples, no secret."

"I—I may not be able to get them all at once," said Jane anxiously. "But I'll have them in a week."

Jane had had another inspiration. She would not eat her apple a day. She would save them up till she had six. Perhaps the doctor might come, but what of it? She liked Dr. Nicholas. He had come to see her when she had been sick in the spring, and he was rosy and jolly and twinkling. He had told her mother and Aunt Helen — especially Aunt Helen — that she must be let live in the sunshine all summer and she would be all right by fall.

"Well, I'll think it over," said Dovie doubtfully. "Don't get your hopes up. I don't expect I'll tell you any secret after all. You're too young I've told you so often enough."

"I'm older than I was last week," pleaded Jane. "Oh,

Dovie, you have so many lovely secrets. You might spare me one. Don't be so mean."

"I guess I've got a right to my own secrets," said Dovie crushingly. "Get a secret of your own, Jane Lawrence, if you want one so much."

"I don't know how," cried Jane in despair, "and it would be so lovely to have a secret."

"Oh, it's wonderful," agreed Dovie. "I tell you, Jane, life isn't worth living without secrets. Six apples isn't much to pay for one. If you'd give me that little gold chain of yours now . . ."

"I couldn't do that," said Jane miserably. "It isn't really mine, you see. It's Mother's, though she lets me wear it sometimes. Father gave it to her just before he died. It's almost the only little bit of jewelry she has."

"Oh, of course I know you and your mother are poor as church mice," agreed Dovie. "Ma says she doesn't know what you'd have done when your mother got sick if your Aunt Helen hadn't taken you in. My, she was mad at having to do it, though. She told Ma her and George had enough to do to make both ends meet as it was. And she said as soon as Hester — that's your ma, you know—"

"Of course I know my own mother's name," said Jane, a trifle on her dignity. Secrets or no secrets, there were limits.

"Well, your Aunt Helen said that she bet as soon as Hester got well again she'd have to go back to her work. What did your ma work at in town, Jane?"

"She taught school," said Jane, "and taught it well. But the secret, Dovie — you'll tell me one, won't you?"

"We'll see when you get those six apples," was all Dovie would say.

But she had never conceded so much before, and Jane's hopes were high.

She continued to sit on the wharf long after Dovie had gone. She liked to sit on the wharf and watch the fishing boats going out and coming in, and sometimes a ship drifting down the harbor, bound to fair lands far away — "far, far away" — Jane repeated the words to herself with a relish. They savored of magic. She wished she could sail away in a ship — down the blue harbor, past the bar of shadowy dunes, past Prospect Point, which at sunset became an outpost of mystery; out, out to the blue mist that was a summer sea; on, on to enchanted islands in golden morning seas. Jane flew on the wings of her imagination all over the world as she squatted there on the old, sagging, half-decayed wharf.

This afternoon she was all keyed up about the secret. Dovie Johnson and she had been playmates of a sort ever since Jane had come to Bartibog. The very first time Jane had ever seen her, Dovie had whispered,

"I know a secret."

That is the most intriguing phrase in the world. From that moment Jane was Dovie's humble and adoring satellite. Dovie liked Jane well enough.

"No harm in her — a bit soft," she told the other Bartibog girls, none of whom bothered much about Jane.

Would Dovie really tell her a secret? And what would it be? Something lovely, of course. Secrets were always lovely. Perhaps Dovie had been through the looking glass like Alice. Or perhaps she had seen a tiny white fairy lying on a lily pad in her father's pond. Or a boat sailing down the Bartibog River, drawn by stately white swans attached to silver chains. Perhaps the secret was something the birds told her. Or it might be that she had been to the moon.

The moon, white and frail, was hanging over the sand dunes now. Soon it would be bright and shining. Jane loved the moon. She loved to dream about it. It was a silver world of fancy where she lived a strange dream life. She never told any one about it, not even Mother, so Jane really had a wonderful secret all her own if she had only had sense enough to know it.

Perhaps Dovie knew a princess. Or, since princesses were scarce in Bartibog, just a common, everyday girl who had been changed into a toad by a witch. But no — Jane shivered — that would not be beautiful, and secrets were always beautiful. Surely Dovie would tell her one. How happy she would be when Dovie had told her a secret! She was happy now in the very thought of it, so happy that even Aunt Helen's frown when she came in late to supper couldn't squelch her.

Anyhow Aunt Helen was always frowning. Jane thought she would be glad for more reasons than one when Mother was well enough to go back to town and teach. Somehow she knew Mother would be very glad, too, though Mother was always sweet and never answered back when Aunt Helen said mean little things. Jane didn't mind—much— when Aunt Helen said mean things to her. But she hated it when she said them to Mother. Mother was so dear and pretty and sad. And not strong. Aunt Helen was always twitting her about that. There must be something wicked about not being strong, though Jane couldn't imagine what it was. She wasn't strong herself.

"But how could she be?" she had heard Aunt Helen saying to Uncle George. "Her mother has no constitution. It was a mistake for Beverley ever to marry her. And the girls he might have had!"

Jane liked to speculate on those girls Father might have had. One of them might have been her mother. But that was horrible. Nobody could be her mother except Mother. The thing was simply unthinkable.

"I think Dovie Johnson is going to tell me a secret," Jane confided to Mother that night when she was being put to bed. "Of course I won't be able to tell it to you, Mother, because no more than two people can have a secret. You won't mind, will you, darling?"

"Not at all," said Mother, much amused.

Dovie Johnson always amused her. George said she was "a young devil," and Helen didn't approve of Jane's playing with her — "though the Johnsons are *very* respectable."

179

But there was no one else for Jane to play with, and she was so taken up with Dovie.

For a week Jane denied herself her daily apple. When Aunt Helen gave it to her — grudgingly, as she gave everything — Jane would slip away, ostensibly to eat it, but in reality to store it in a box in the granary. She watched the apples anxiously for spot or blemish. Those apples didn't keep. But when she met Dovie on the wharf the next Saturday morning, she had the six apples, fair and unmarred.

"Here are the apples, Dovie," she said breathlessly. "And now tell me the secret."

Dovie looked at the apples rather disdainfully. "They're small," she said.

Jane's heart sank. "They're *all* small this summer," she faltered.

Dovie pursed up her lips. "I'll tell you the secret some other time."

"I don't want to hear it some other time," cried Jane. Jane had a spirit of her own, and nothing roused it more quickly than injustice. "A bargain is a bargain, Dovie Johnson. You *said* six apples for a secret. Here are the apples. And you shan't have a bite unless you tell me the secret."

"Oh, very well," said Dovie in a bored way. "Only don't blame me if you don't like it so well when you hear it. Swear you'll never tell any one, cross your heart and hope to die."

"Of course I won't tell. It wouldn't be a secret then."

"Well, listen," said Dovie.

Jane listened. The water swelling around the piers of the wharf listened. The hills across the harbor listened. Or so it seemed to Jane. The whole world was listening. Jane shivered with delicious ecstasy. She was going to hear a secret at last.

"You know the Jimmy Thomases down at the Harbor Mouth?" said Dovie. Six-toed Jimmy Thomas?"

Jane nodded. Of course she knew the Jimmy Thomases — at least, knew of them. Uncle George got his fish from them. But what could they possibly have to do with the secret?

"And you know Ellen Thomas?" went on Dovie.

Jane had seen Ellen Thomas once, when Six-toed Jimmy had brought her round with him in his fish wagon. She had not liked her much. Ellen was just about her own age, with jet-black bobbed hair and bold black eyes. She had stuck her tongue out at Jane.

"Well—" Dovie drew a long breath — "this is the secret. *You* are Ellen Thomas, and *she* is Jane Lawrence."

Jane stared at Dovie. She hadn't the faintest glimmer of Dovie's meaning. What she had said made no sense.

"I—I—what do you mean?"

"It's plain enough, I should think." Dovie smiled pityingly. "You and her was born the same night. It was when your ma and your dad were living in that little house at the Harbor Head when he was working for the Biligy people. The nurse took you down to Thomases' and put you in Ellen's cradle and brought Ellen back to your ma. Nobody but her ever knew the difference. She did it because she hated your ma. She wanted your dad for herself, and she took that way of getting even. And that is why you are really Ellen Thomas, and you ought to be living down there at the Harbor Mouth, and poor Jane Lawrence ought to be up at your Uncle George's instead of being banged about by that stepmother of hers."

Jane believed every word of this preposterous yarn. Not for one moment did she doubt the truth of Dovie's tale. She gazed at Dovie with anguished, disillusioned eyes. This —*this* was the beautiful secret!

"How—how did you find out?" she gasped through dry lips.

"The nurse told me on her deathbed," said Dovie solemnly. "I s'pose her conscience troubled her. I've never told any one. The next time I saw Ellen Thomas — Jane

Lawrence, I mean — I took a good look at her. She has just the same kind of ears as your ma. And she's dark complected like your ma. *You*'ve got blue eyes and yellow hair. I don't s'pose anything can be done about it now. But I've often thought it wasn't fair, you having such an easy time, and your ma keeping you like a doll, and poor El—Jane in rags and not getting enough to eat many's the time. And old Six-toed beating her when he comes home drunk. Say, these apples are dandy." Dovie took a huge bite out of one. "If you'll give me six more next week, I'll tell you another secret."

"I don't want to hear any more," cried Jane passionately. She could never forget what she *had* heard. Her pain was greater than she could bear. "I *hate* you for telling me this, Dovie Johnson."

Dovie shrugged. "I told you you mightn't like it, didn't I? Where are you going?"

For Jane, white and dizzy, had risen to her feet. "Home, to tell Mother," she said miserably.

"You mustn't—you dasn't. Remember, you swore you wouldn't tell any one," cried Dovie. "The Black Man will get you if you do."

Jane didn't know who the Black Man was and didn't care. But it was true, she promised not to tell. And Mother always said you must never break a promise.

"I guess I'll be getting home myself," said Dovie, not altogether liking the look of Jane.

She gathered up her apples and ran off, her bare dusty legs twinkling along the old wharf. Behind her she left a broken-hearted child sitting among the ruins of her small universe. Dovie didn't care. Jane was such a softy, it really wasn't much fun to fool her.

Jane sat on the wharf for what seemed hours — blind, crushed, despairing. She wasn't Mother's child; she was Six-toed Jimmy's child — Six-toed Jimmy, of whom she had always had such a secret dread simply because of his six toes. She had no business to be living with Mother, loved by Mother. Oh! Jane gave a piteous little moan. Mother wouldn't love her any more if she knew. All her love would go to Ellen Thomas. And yet she—*she,* Jane Lawrence—was Ellen Thomas.

Jane put her hand to her head. "It makes me dizzy."

"What's the reason you ain't eating nothing?" asked Aunt Helen sharply at the dinner table.

"Were you out in the sun too long, darling?" said Mother anxiously. "Does your head ache?"

"Ye—es," said Jane. Something *was* aching terribly, but it didn't seem to be her head. Was she telling a lie to Mother? And if so, how many more would she have to tell? For Jane knew she would never be able to eat again — never so long as this horrible secret was hers. And she knew she could never tell Mother. Not so much because of the promise — Jane had heard Aunt Helen say that a bad promise was better broken than kept — but because it would hurt Mother. Somehow Jane knew beyond any doubt that it would hurt Mother horribly. And Mother mustn't, shouldn't, be hurt. Jane recalled the time she had heard Mother crying in the night. She could never forget it. She must never breathe the secret to Mother.

And yet, there was Ellen Thomas. She wouldn't call her Jane Lawrence. It made Jane feel awful beyond any description to think of Ellen Thomas as being Jane Lawrence. She felt as if it blotted her out altogether. If she wasn't Jane Lawrence, she wasn't anybody. She would *not* be Ellen Thomas.

But Ellen Thomas haunted her. For a week Jane was beset by her — a wretched, wretched week during which Mother worried herself almost sick over Jane, who wouldn't eat and wouldn't play with Dovie Johnson any more and, just as Aunt Helen scornfully said, "moped around." Mother would have sent for Dr. Nicholas, but Dr. Nicholas was away for his vacation, and his practice was being looked after by some strange doctor who was boarding at the Harbor Hotel, and Aunt Helen didn't hold with strange doctors.

Jane had often wondered why, when people came to Bartibog for vacation, Dr. Nicholas should go away for his. But now Jane wondered over nothing except the one awful question which had emerged from her confusion of mind and taken possession of her. Shouldn't Ellen Thomas have her rights? Was it fair that she, Jane Lawrence — Jane clung to her own identity frantically — should have all the things that Ellen Thomas was denied and which were hers by rights? No, it wasn't fair. Jane was despairingly sure it wasn't fair. Somewhere in Jane there was a very strong sense of justice and fair play. And it became increasingly borne in upon her that it was only fair that Ellen Thomas should be told. After all, she didn't suppose Mother would care so much. She would be a little upset at first, of course, but as soon as she knew that Ellen Thomas was really her own child, all her love would go to Ellen, and Jane would become of no account to her. Mother would kiss Ellen Thomas and sing to her in the twilight when the fog was coming in from the sea — sing the song Jane loved best:

"I saw a ship a-sailing, a-sailing on the sea,
And, oh, it was all laden with pretty things for me."

Jane and Mother had often talked about the time their ship would come in. But now the pretty things would be Ellen Thomas'.

There came a day when Jane knew she could bear it no longer. She must do what was fair. She would go down to the Harbor Mouth — it was only a mile — and tell the Thomases the truth. They could tell Mother. Jane felt that she simply could not do that.

Jane felt a little better when she had come to this decision; better, but very, very sad. She tried to eat a little at supper because it would be the last meal she would ever eat with Mother.

"I'll always call her 'Mother'," thought Jane desperately. "And I won't call Six-toed Jimmy 'Father.' I'll just say,

184

'Mr. Thomas' very respectfully. Surely he won't mind that.''

But something choked her. She couldn't eat. Again Mother said timidly she wished she could see the doctor at the hotel.

"Dr. Nicholas will be back next week," said Aunt Helen. "We don't know a thing about that doctor at the hotel, not even his name. And his bill would likely be terrible. There isn't any great rush. You're always worrying over Jane. She runs around too much. That's all that ails her.''

"She hasn't run around much lately," said Mother, standing up to Aunt Helen in a way she seldom dared to.

Her eyes sparkled, and a little flush stained her soft round cheeks that had been pale so long. Jane looked at Mother, suddenly seeing her for the first time. Before this she had just been Mother — somebody who cuddled and kissed you and looked after you and comforted you. All at once she had become a different person. Why, Mother was young and pretty — very pretty. She had beautiful soft dark eyes with long lashes, beautiful black hair in little waves about her face. Black hair! Jane's heart was torn by another pang. Ellen Thomas had black hair. Of course. Wasn't she Mother's daughter? Jane herself was fair — "like Beverley," Aunt Helen had said. Only unluckily she had never said it in Jane's hearing.

Nothing came of Mother's little flare-up. Aunt Helen was unmoved. Jane knew that Mother had to be patient until she was strong enough to go back to work.

Jane went right off after supper. She must go before it was dark, or her courage would fail her. Mother and Aunt Helen thought she was going to the wharf to play with Dovie. But Jane walked right past the wharf and down the harbor road, a gallant, indomitable little figure. Jane had no notion that she was a heroine. On the contrary, she felt very much ashamed of herself because it was so hard to do what was right and fair, so hard to keep from hating Ellen Thomas, so hard to keep from fearing Six-toed Jimmy, so

185

hard to keep from turning round and running back to Mother.

It was a lowering evening. Out to sea were heavy black clouds. Fitful lightning played over the harbor and the dark wooded hills beyond it. The village of fishermen's houses at the Harbor Mouth lay flooded in a red light that escaped from under the low-hung clouds. Dozens of children were playing on the sand. They looked curiously at Jane when she stopped to ask which was Six-toed Jimmy's house.

"That one over there," said a boy, pointing. "What's your business with him?"

"Thank you," said Jane, turning away.

"Have ye got no more manners than that?" yelled a girl. "Too stuck up to answer a civil question."

The boy got in front of her. "See that house back of Thomases'?" he said. "It's full of rats, and I'll lock you up in it if you don't tell me what you want with Six-toed Jimmy."

"Come, now, behave like a lady," said a big girl tauntingly. "You're from Bartibog, and the Bartibogers all think they're the cheese. Answer Bill's question."

"If you don't, look out," said another boy. "I'm going to drown some kittens, and I'm quite likely to pop you in, too."

"If you've got a dime about you, I'll sell you a tooth," said a red-headed girl, grinning. "I had one pulled yesterday."

"I haven't a dime, and your tooth would be no use to me," said Jane, plucking up a little spirit. "You let me alone."

"None of your lip," said Redhead.

Jane started to run. The rat boy stuck out a foot and tripped her up. She fell her length on the tide-rippled sand. The others screamed with laughter. But some one exclaimed,

"There's Blue Jack's boat coming in."

186

Away they all ran. Jane picked herself up. Her dress was plastered with sand, and her stockings were soiled. But she was free from her tormentors. Would these be her playmates in the future?

She must not cry; she must not. She climbed the rickety board steps that led up to Six-toed Jimmy's door. Like all the harbor houses, Six-toed Jimmy's was raised on blocks of wood to be out of reach of any unusually high tide, and the space underneath it was filled with a medley of broken dishes, empty cans, old lobster traps, and all kinds of rubbish. The door was open, and Jane looked into a kitchen the like of which she had never seen in her life. The bare floor was dirty. The sink was full of dirty dishes. The remains of a meal were on a rickety old wooden table, and horrid big black flies were swarming over it. A woman with an untidy mop of grayish hair was sitting on a rocker nursing a baby — a baby gray with dirt.

"*My sister*," thought Jane.

There was no sign of Ellen or Six-toed Jimmy, for which latter fact Jane felt thankful.

"Who are you, and what do you want?" said the woman rather ungraciously.

She did not ask Jane in, but Jane walked in. It was beginning to rain outside, and a peal of thunder made the house shake. Jane knew she must say what she had come to say before her courage failed her, or she would turn and run from that dreadful house and that dreadful baby and those dreadful flies.

"I want to see Ellen, please," she said. "I have something important to tell her."

"Indeed, now!" said the woman. "It must be important from the size of you. Well, Ellen isn't home. Her dad took her up to West Bartibog for a ride, and with this storm coming up there's no telling when they'll be back. Sit down."

Jane sat down on the broken chair. She had known the harbor folks were poor, but she had not known any of them were like this. She had once been in Mrs. Tom Fitch's house with Uncle George, and it was as neat and tidy as Aunt Helen's. Of course, every one knew that Six-toed Jimmy drank up everything he made. And this was to be her home henceforth!

"Anyhow I'll try to clean it up," thought Jane forlornly, but her heart was like lead; the flame of high self-sacrifice which had lured her on was gone out.

"What are you wanting to see Ellen for?" asked Mrs. Six-toed curiously. "If it's about that Sunday school picnic, she can't go — that's flat. She hasn't a decent rag. How can I get her any, I ask you?"

"No, it's not about the picnic," said Jane drearily. She might as well tell Mrs. Thomas the whole story. She would have to know it anyhow. "I came to tell her—to tell her that—that she is me, and I'm her."

Perhaps Mrs. Six-toed might be forgiven for not thinking this very lucid. "Are you cracked?" she exclaimed. "Whatever on earth do you mean?"

Jane lifted her head. The worst was over now. "I mean that Ellen and I were born the same night, and—and—the nurse changed us because she had a spite at Mother, and —and—Ellen ought to be living with Mother and—and— having advantages."

That last phrase was one of Aunt Helen's, but Jane thought it made a dignified ending to a very lame speech.

Mrs. Six-toed stared at her. "Am I crazy, or are you? What you've been saying doesn't make any sense. Whoever told you such a rigmarole?"

"Dovie Johnson."

Mrs. Six-toed threw back her tousled head and laughed. She might be dirty and draggled, but she had an attractive laugh. "I might have knowed it. That's Dovie all over, the young imp. Well, little Miss What's-your-name, you'd better not be believing all Dovie's yarns, or she'll lead you a merry dance."

"Do you mean it isn't true?" gasped Jane.

"Not very likely. You must be pretty green to fall for anything like that. Ellen's a good six months older than you. Who on earth are you, anyhow?"

"I'm Jane Lawrence." Oh, beautiful thought, she *was* Jane Lawrence!

"Jane Lawrence! Beverley Lawrence's little girl? Why, I remember the night you were born. I was down at the Biology Station helping out in the house. I wasn't married to Six-toed then — more's the pity I ever was — and Ellen's mother was living and healthy. I knew your dad well. A nice young fellow he was, even if he didn't live long. You look like him — you've got his eyes and hair. And to think you'd no more sense than to fall for that crazy yarn of Dovie's!"

"I am in the habit of believing people," said Jane, rising with a slight stateliness of manner, but too deliriously happy to want to snub Mrs. Six-toed very sharply.

"Well, it's a habit you'd better get out of when you're round with any of the Johnson tribe," said Mrs. Six-toed. "Sit down, child. You can't go home till this storm's over. It's pouring rain and dark as a stack of black cats. Why, she's gone — the child's gone!"

Jane was already blotted out in the downpour. Nothing but the wild exultation born of Mrs. Six-toed's words could have carried her home through that storm. The wind buffeted her, the rain streamed upon her; only the constant glare of the lightning showed her the road. Again and again she slipped and fell. Once she cut her wrist on a sliver of broken glass. But at last she reeled, dripping, mud-plastered, blood-stained, into the kitchen at Uncle George's, where Mother, as pale as ashes, was pacing frantically up and down. Even Aunt Helen was looking disturbed.

Mother ran and caught Jane in her arms. "Darling, what a fright you have given us! Oh, where have you been?"

"I only hope your Uncle George won't get his death out

in this rain searching for you," said Aunt Helen, but there was some shrewish relief in her voice.

Jane had almost had the breath battered out of her. She could only gasp as she felt Mother's dear arms enfolding her:

"Oh, Mother, I'm me, really me. I'm not Ellen Thomas."

"That child is delirious," said Aunt Helen. "Well, it's a very inconvenient time for her to be sick."

Much water had flowed under Bartibog Bridge before the October day when Dovie Johnson held a group of girls spellbound on the school playground while she told them a secret.

"Of course, everybody will soon know it. Jane's mother is going to be married to Dr. Oswald King. It's all very romantic. When Jane was so sick the morning after that thunderstorm in July, her mother just went haywire and vowed she would have the doctor from the hotel, Mrs. George or no Mrs. George. They didn't even know his name, but when he came — what do you think? He was an old beau of Mrs. Lawrence's, and she had liked him real well, too, only she liked Bev Lawrence better. But Dr. King never liked any one else, and he had never married. And now he's going to marry Mrs. Lawrence in a week's time. I'll bet she'll be glad to get away from Mrs. Second-skimmings!"

"How will Jane like it?" asked a girl. "She's always been so wrapped up in her mother."

"Oh, Dr. King was so good to her all the time she was getting over the pneumonia that she's just crazy about him. They're going to take her on their honeymoon in Europe. And when they come back, Jane's going to a very private and 'sclusive school in Halifax. I'm glad of her luck. I always liked Jane, though she was a bit soft! That kid would believe anything you told her!"

BOOKS BY L. M. MONTGOMERY

COLLECTED SHORT STORIES

Chronicles of Avonlea, 1910.
Further Chronicles of Avonlea, 1920.
The Road to Yesterday, 1974.

NOVELS

Anne of Green Gables, 1908.
Anne of Avonlea, 1909.
Kilmeny of the Orchard, 1910.
The Story Girl, 1911.
The Golden Road, 1913.
Anne of the Island, 1915.
Anne's House of Dreams, 1917.
Rilla of Ingleside, 1921.
Emily of New Moon, 1923.
Rainbow Valley, 1925.
Emily Climbs, 1925.
The Blue Castle, 1926.
Emily's Quest, 1927.
Magic for Marigold, 1929.
A Tangled Web, 1931 (English edition under the title
Aunt Becky Began).
Pat of Silver Bush, 1932.
Mistress Pat, 1935.
Anne of Windy Poplars, 1936 (Canadian edition under
the title *Anne of Windy Willows*).
Jane of Lantern Hill, 1937.

ESSAYS

With Marian Keith and Mabel Burns McKinley,
Courageous Women, 1934.

AUTOBIOGRAPHY

*The Alpine Path: The Story of My Career, Everywoman's
World*, 1974 (reprinted from *Everywoman's World*,
June to November 1917).

LETTERS

The Green Gables Letters From L. M. Montgomery to Ephraim Weber, 1905-1909, edited by Wilfred Eggleston, 1960.

DRAMA

Anne of Green Gables, adapted by Alice Chadwicke, 1937. *Anne of Green Gables,* musical, written and composed by Donald Harron and Normal Campbell, 1965.

BOOKS AND ARTICLES ON L. M. MONTGOMERY

Anonymous. *Lucy Maud Montgomery, The Island's Lady of Stories.* Women's Institute, Springfield, Charlottetown, 1964.

Bolger, Francis P. *The Years Before "Anne."* Prince Edward Island Heritage Foundation, 1974.

Gillen, Mollie. *The Wheel of Things, A Biography of L. M. Montgomery.* Toronto: Fitzhenry and Whiteside, 1975; also: "Maud Montgomery: The Girl Who Wrote Green Gables," in *Chatelaine* 46, July 1973.

Hill, Maude Petit, "The Best Known Woman in Prince Edward Island," *Chatelaine,* May and June 1928.

Ridley, Hilda M. *The Story of L. M. Montgomery,* Toronto: Ryerson, 1956.

Sclanders, Ian, "Lucy of Green Gables," *Maclean's Magazine* 64, Dec. 15, 1951.

Sorflect, John, ed. *Canadian Children's Literature* (L. M. Montgomery Issue), vol. 1, no. 3, Autumn 1975.

Waterson, Elizabeth. "Lucy Maud Montgomery," in *The Clear Spirit: Twenty Canadian Women and Their Times,* ed. Mary Quayle Innis. Toronto: University of Toronto Press, 1966.

Waller, Adrian, "Lucy Maud Montgomery," in *Readers' Digest* (Canada), Dec. 1975, pp. 38-43.

Weber, Ephraim, "L. M. Montgomery's Anne," *Dalhousie Review* 24, April 1944, pp. 64-73.